PAULETTE POUJOL ORIOL

VALE

OF

TEARS

A NOVEL FROM HAITI

FOREWORD BY EDWIDGE DANTICAT
TRANSLATED BY DOLORES A. SCHAEFER

IBEX PUBLISHERS
Bethesda, Maryland

VALE OF TEARS, A NOVEL FROM HAITI
translation of *Le Passage* from the French by Dolores A. Schaefer

Manufactured in the United States of America

The paper used in this book meets the minimum requirements of the American National Standard for Information Services - Permanence of Paper for Printed Library Materials, ANSI Z39.48-1984

Ibex Publishers, Inc.
Post Office Box 30087
Bethesda, Maryland 20824
Telephone: 301-718-8188
Facsimile: 301-907-8707
www.ibexpublishers.com

LIBRARY OF CONGRESS CATALOGING-IN-PUBLICATION INFORMATION

Poujol Oriol, Paulette.
[Passage. English]
Vale of tears : a novel / Paulette Poujol Oriol ; translation of Le passage from the French by Dolores A. Schaefer ; foreword by Edwidge Danticat.
p. cm.
ISBN 1588140202 (alk. paper)
1. Schaefer, Dolores A.   II. Title.

PQ3949.2.P63 P3713 2005
843/.914 22 — dc22
2004065760

FOREWORD

Journeys, internal or external, physical or psychological, are among literature's most engaging and fascinating themes. From *Don Quixote* to *Gulliver's Travels*, quest narratives have always linked trying pilgrimages with potentially life-changing revelations for both their characters and the readers. So it is with the journey of Coralie, the main character of Paulette Poujol Oriol's *Vale of Tears*, the first of her many remarkable novels to be published in English.

Here, in equally suspenseful parallel narratives, we follow Coralie at two different stages of her life, first as a young woman who is expelled from Catholic school for making an inadvertently sexual remark, then as an older woman who is going from house to house looking for handouts. The younger woman's narrative tells of how after her expulsion, she enters a loveless marriage then following her husband's death abandons her infant son in Haiti to move to Europe where she engages in a series of dangerous liaisons, including one with a Nazi officer. When she finally returns to Haiti, eight years after her departure, she finds that most of the fortune she had inherited from her husband has been pilfered and she has no choice but to accept a meager allowance from her relatives and become involved with men who support her in return for sexual favors.

As the dual strands of the narrative are woven together, we watch Coralie's fall become more and more humiliating, when she is forced to beg old friends and family members for food and car fare on New Year's Eve of all times. During what is supposed to be a time of renewal, she finds herself unable to surface from an ongoing nightmare, which connects her fate to that of millions of poor Haitians, whose circumstances have always been bleak. As Coralie's journey progresses, we slowly come to realize that what is keeping her alive are tiny acts of kindness from the least expected sources and colorful memories of her adventurous past, memories which slowly fade into the ugliness of a present she can no longer avoid.

Oriol's genius is that she makes this single life seem doubly epic. It would have been simple enough to show Coralie unraveling, however, we are moved to feel both anger and compassion towards Coralie, in part because she witnesses so many larger tragedies firsthand, World War II for example, and never seems to learn from them. That is until it is too late. Getting to know both the older Coralie and the younger one at the same time underscores the many tribulations of this life and is one more thing that keeps us glued to these beautifully crafted pages.

What a remarkable accomplishment for the writer that we can both love and hate Coralie at the same time and still grieve when the inevitable happens as though she were an old friend we had care-lessly neglected when she needed us most. This book is a wonderful introduction to Ms. Oriol's work for English-speaking readers. Hopefully there will be more translations of her other books and we will have the privilege of taking other journeys with her.

Edwidge Danticat

To my dearly beloved husband, Marc Oriol,
for all he has given me and for even more than that ...

If life is a path,
at least we can sow flowers on it.
Fançois Paradis de Moncrif (1687-1770)

INTRODUCTORY REMARKS

This novel is an answer to a question asked by a very dear friend who wanted to know why my hero, Pierre Tervil, in my earlier novel, *Le Creuset*, always maintains such an upward moral and social momentum and why everything seems to succeed in his life. I answered her in 1981 "I could just as well have painted a character who fails."

It is to this friend, who recently died after an excruciating illness, that I dedicate the shadowy figure of the heroine in this novel, Coralie Santeuil.

Paulette Poujol Oriol

ONE

"Cora-a-a-a-lie! Co-ra-a-a-li-e!"

The little girl at the far end of the immense garden stops playing. She had been running like the wind, a paper pinwheel in her right hand, a cloth doll with a porcelain head and feet tucked under her left arm. This doll is Jeannette, her daughter, the one her dear Papa gave her last Christmas. She is beautiful with long, silky brown hair. Coralie wanted to show Jeannette the big rosebush with yellow flowers that she often kisses, loving the feel on her lips of the velvety petals and the morning dew. Coralie is in no hurry to go back to the big, white house with its round pillars where her young stepmother, Aline Santeuil, stands with a threatening lash in her hand.

Coralie hates this harsh little woman with the pointed nose. Her stepmother looks like a mouse. She has piercing little eyes that don't miss a thing. So today she knew, she found out right away, that Coralie, instead of studying her catechism lesson, had slipped away to the far end of the garden with her paper windmill and above all with her doll, her Jeannette. The little minx had planned her mischief well. Coralie had spied on her stepmother working in the pantry with the cook, Idamise. And then she tiptoed to Aline's bedroom. Quickly grabbing a chair, she leaned against the armoire on top of which Aline had put Jeannette to punish Coralie. Jeannette, her pretty doll she gets to play with just once each week after Sunday dinner. An entire, long week without her daughter. Coralie looks for every opportunity to take back her toy. Punished each time, she does it all over again anyway. Right now, her whole body is shaking. All she wanted to do was give Jeannette a whiff of fresh air, show Jeannette her favorite rosebush, the one with such beautiful yellow roses, and help her see how the butterflies dancing in the changing air are like living flowers. But how can she explain that to Aline who is waiting for her with a lash in her hand? Coralie knows that thanks to her escapade, she will spend three whole weeks without seeing her doll. The whip hurts, but it is over fast. You cry and then you forget. But the lengthy separation from her child, that is what the seven-year old girl cannot stand. That is why she is going to beg for forgiveness so that her punishment might be shortened.

She slowly approaches her angry stepmother.

"Mama, I'm deeply sorry," she begins.

Then it is horrible. Aline grabs the doll with a rough gesture, bangs it against the banister, and Jeannette's head flies in shiny fragments that scatter on the tile floor. Choking from the shock, Coralie does not cry right away. Her mouth open, she searches for her breath, and when she finds it, she lets out a wail that comes from deep inside of her. Drawn by the cries, Mr. Santeuil appears at the door of his library. He is always calm, but today he is stunned because he does not recognize his daughter. Like an enraged cat, Coralie throws herself at Aline, pummeling her with awkward blows. She scratches, she bites, she is wild, a howling little beast carried off to the first floor by the servants.

Coldly, calmly, Aline takes her husband's arm. "I told you, my dear," she says, "that this child is becoming uncontrollable. It's about time we sent her to boarding school."

THE FIRST STATION

DECEMBER 31: WANEY

6:00 A.M.

Coralie Santeuil stretches her long, thin body out on the creaky wharf. A ray of sunshine slips through a crack between two planks, dust dancing a golden saraband in it. The shaft of blond light falls on the sleeping woman's left eye. With her hand she tries to brush it aside like a buzzing fly. The sun teases her forehead. She turns over in search of a shady spot where the light will not rob her of the pleasure of her dreamy state. If only she could simply never wake up.

Lazily Coralie finally opens one eye, then the other, and looks at the bank calendar hanging on the dirty wall opposite her bed. December 31, the end of the month, the end of the year, the end of everything.

She slowly sits up on her bed, the straw-filled mattress squeaking under her weight. She places her pointed elbows on her bony knees. Wisps of gray hair hang down alongside her hollow, ash-colored cheeks. She raises herself slowly and painfully stands up. Leaning forward, her body sways before gaining its balance. She remains standing in the same place for a while, then approaches the wrought-iron stand holding her enameled wash basin crowned with lime deposits. The basin's rounded edges are rusty where the enamel is chipped. On the floor sits a gray-green tin pail containing yellow water covered with a thin film of dust. Using a dirty, dull pink plastic goblet, she scoops up a little water to splash on her face. She then looks at herself for a long time in the mirror which hangs on the partition above the basin. She sees three triangular Coralies, fragments of sad, dejected faces, reflected in the angular, broken pieces of the mirror lodged in its metal frame. She shakes her head, closes her eyes, then returns to her bed, her walk strange and dejected. Her body rocks when she moves about, and she always seems on the verge of falling.

Stretched out, she lets her mind wander to December 31, the last day of the year, the last day of the month. Today she must find the money for her small room. She absolutely must have it. Yesterday the owner of this shack and all the others in this shanty-town, Waney, notified her about paying without fail by January 1 at the very latest or she would have to *"kale m' kay mwen,* get the hell out of my house." She owes six months' rent. God, how is she going to pay? By what miracle is she going to find the one hundred dollars she owes her dreadful landlord? She must pay the six months due plus a six-month advance to be left in peace until next June. She will have to walk, walk, walk as far as her sons' houses. Her sons....

Then Coralie closes her eyes. A couple of tears fall on the coarse unbleached cotton pillowcase. She predicts her sons' welcome. They are so ashamed of her—the reprobate, the shameful one, the street vagabond, Cora the abject, worthless, debased being she has become over the years, a pitiful creature, a beggar, one of those abandoned souls to whom people give money without daring to look them in the eyes.

With her good hand, she gathers up the long, grayish wisps of hair that hang around her disfigured face, knotting them into a tight chignon. Holding between her teeth the rubber band that is to keep them in place, she slips on her best dress, the one Mrs. Dieufils gave her two years ago. The dark, hand-me-down dress, a *pèpè* with green flowers hangs from her skinny shoulders as if from a metal coat hanger. She washes her feet, slips on her clear, plastic sandals, and takes a faded, yellow handbag from the pine table beside her bed. In it she puts an empty coin purse, a comb with only its large teeth intact, and a fine batiste handkerchief which has seen better days. Despite hundreds of washings, a coat of arms still bears witness to a long-lost, prosperous period never to be seen again.

From the doorway, she takes in at a glance the little bedroom she is leaving. Will she return later with the precious rent money, or will she be thrown into the street tomorrow with her worn-out clothing, chipped washbasin, broken mirror, and the outdated calendar pictures that decorate the clay walls? Sighing, she closes the disjointed wood door whose harsh groan now seems to be the most agreeable noise in the world. Until today, she has at least had a place of her own, a roof, a shelter. She is now at the end of her rope. Nothing, nothing at all, not even hope. Alone, facing this empty road she must take, she has to begin her search. Now she has to walk. Walk where?

She sighs, "Félix ... Robert..." and plunges into December's cold sunlight.

TWO

Félicien Santeuil was an important wholesale merchant from Rue du Quai. The son of an influential family educated in the best schools, he had made several trips to Europe where he specialized in the trade of French wine and English soap. There was not an upper-class table that Santeuil, an importer of the best vintages, did not supply. At all official and family receptions, people owed it to themselves to serve Santeuil's wines. His store, divided into two parts, welcomed both gentlemen tempted by a good bottle and women needing a box of lavender, violet, or lettuce extract soap for a gift or their own use. The House of Santeuil catered only to the wealthiest clients, and Félicien got reasonably rich in the process.

Late in life he married a pretty woman from Cap Haitien, a quadroon as blond as an ear of corn and as fragile as a flower, who died two years after their marriage while giving birth to Coralie. Félicien was not a man who cried for long about lost love. He had several adventures in the early states of his widowhood, passing affairs without emotional attachment. He was ready prey for Aline Marceau, the daughter of his sales director, Benoît Marceau, a man of integrity totally devoted to his boss. No sooner had Mr. Santeuil become a widower than Aline, barely twenty years old, worked her way into the store on the pretext of helping her father. She had beautiful handwriting, and at a time when copies of letters were done by hand, she became a kind of volunteer secretary for Félicien who adopted the habit of asking her for a letter, a lost paper, a memorandum to fill out quickly, a bill to check. She quickly made herself indispensable to Félicien who found it quite natural to accept the assistance of this educated young lady, twenty years his junior whose freshness and seriousness compensated for her lack of beauty. That is how one fine day Aline found herself the manager of Santeuil's store. Short, thin, and tough as a vine stem compared to her father and her husband, she directed the business with formidable efficiency. She had no equal when it came to checking stock, knowing when to order or not to order, disposing of slightly stale wine in the most advantageous way, and especially in bringing in money owed by recalcitrant debtors. Her steadfast presence in the store and her hold on domestic matters made her extremely precious to Félicien Santeuil, who by nature somewhat indolent beneath his severe appearance, relied more and more on Aline for the smooth running of his commercial and private affairs.

Aline ruled with an iron rod and knew how to make everyone obey her. So she was all the more upset with Coralie who, from the beginning of her marriage, had seemed a burdensome responsibility she wanted to get rid of sooner or later. As a baby, the little girl had been more or less entrusted to an old servant, Filo. That worked until Coralie was four years old. At this difficult age for children, when they confront the adult world with contempt and defiance and at a time when Coralie needed more and more tenderness and understanding, Aline showed only severity and rejected the little girl who, Aline thought, was stubborn and disobedient. They were at loggerheads. Nothing the little girl did found favor in Aline's eyes. Coralie did not like and would never like her stepmother. Aline decided that the child should call her "Mama" and every time this word came out of Coralie's mouth, it took a big effort, and she said it against her will. Rather than having to call a stepmother she hated and who mistreated her "Mama," Coralie developed the habit of talking to the servants or keeping quiet if all else failed. Félicien, immersed in his euphoria, did not notice that his daughter was becoming somber and withdrawn. He found her obedient and well-mannered and gave all the credit to his strict wife who incidentally did not miss the chance to play up the smallest difficulty as proof of her know-how and the perfect upbringing she provided for her stepdaughter.

The mistreatment reached its zenith when Coralie was seven years old. At this time, Aline, after six childless years of marriage, happily gave birth to a son she worshipped beyond belief. Poor Coralie saw herself once and for all treated scarcely better than the servants. Aline would not stop until she got rid of the little hypocrite who would give her "vices" to Marceau, her beloved son, whom she had chosen to name after her own father thus uniting two generations and two family names. And Aline made sure that their only son would inherit Félicien's entire fortune.

The great, bright house decorated with ornamental openwork from Bois Verna, became a hellish prison for little Coralie who could not get away with anything. She was punished for the slightest offense with punches, slaps, or spankings. When she had toys, they were confiscated; she wore her pretty dresses only on rare occasions; her beautiful blond hair was barely combed, and when Aline did it, she pulled out more than half of it. To please Madame, the servants vied with one another to martyr Coralie. Only old Filo, who had raised her, showed some furtive tenderness. Filo had been Félicien's nanny, and Aline did not dare attack her. But Filo was old, very old, and she died before Coralie was eight. Félicien, blinded by his wife, did not understand his little girl's despair when she refused to eat for days on end. The child wasted away, became unattractive and withdrawn, and Aline made a point of emphasizing to her husband that Coralie was a heartless little girl who preferred an old servant to her parents.

Every evening, Coralie's stepmother forced her to give a full account of her day, and she was always punished for the slightest transgression. Annoyed, yet relying on his wife who outsmarted him, Felicien, who wanted peace in his home, began to come around to Aline's point of view that someday soon Coralie would have to be put into a boarding school. The broken doll incident was the last straw. The following week, Coralie was taken to a boarding school run by the Sisters of the Visitation. The poor little girl, barely eight years old, was strangely relieved to spend her first calm day without Aline's shrill voice shattering her eardrums.

So Coralie grew up in boarding school, rarely visited by her stepmother, even more rarely by her father, who seemed to rely completely on what Aline decided. In the dark, dreary Convent of the Visitation, Coralie's only consolation was her friendship with Rose Darcey and Lise Alphonsin, who, with Coralie, made up the trio of "bad eggs" who always had to be constrained, tormented, punished, blamed, and exposed to the ridicule of the other girls, either for their deplorable conduct, according to Sister Elvire, or for their pitiful school work, according to Miss Yvonne.

Miss Yvonne was a small, stunted-looking woman as inflexible as a cudgel, an exceedingly emaciated woman with skinny legs. She was the prototype of the callous old maid who became a teacher through her failure to get married even to the first male who happened along. Her fits of anger were legendary, and made her two, big, bulging eyes literally pop out of her head. With exposed claws she would swoop down on the unhappy child who had the misfortune to displease her, all the while spewing forth vulgarities that cracked the varnish on the facade she put on for the sisters.

Coralie, Rose, and Lise were scared stiff of Miss Yvonne and, terrorized by this shrew who taught them, their school work suffered until they were at the bottom of the class. Exasperated, Miss Yvonne created a day for publicly humiliating these dunces. She called on them to be whipped, not through their heavy uniforms, but on their backsides exposed for everyone to see.

Rose submitted, moaning through the humiliating ordeal, but without wiggling as much as Lise, who fought vigorously. But when Coralie's turn came, her reaction was frenzied, for unlike Rose, who wore easily removed panties with buttons, or Lise, who wore panties with elastic waistbands, Miss Yvonne was unable to find Coralie's buttocks easily. Holding with one hand the wiggling, inverted body of a gesticulating Coralie and taking off her underpants which were held on with a chord was a risky situation Miss Yvonne could not pull off without having one of her pets get a pair of scissors to quickly cut the little chord that held the troublesome undergarment in place. Then Miss Yvonne, exasperated by her overly long wait, as well as by the side-splitting laughter of thirty young ladies enjoying themselves, attacked Coralie's posterior with rage as Coralie tried to bite her torturer's hand. The wood ruler rose and fell with all the more furor as Coralie squirmed kou vètè nan kim savon, like a worm in soapy water, so that Yvonne missed one out of every three blows. Finally, the exhausted school teacher stopped hitting, surprised at the state of the young girl tinged with blood who looked at her, lips tight, brow obstinate, refusing to whimper or cry.

"Impudent creature, I'll tame you," panted Yvonne, shocked just the same by her handiwork. "I'll tame you," she hissed again as her skinny chest slowly quieted down. "Come here."

And then she took the three girls by the hand one after the other and placed them at the classroom door, a sign with an enormous zero attached to their backs facing the corridor where the eleven other boarding school classes were to pass in a few minutes. At their feet, witness to their supreme shame and humiliation, were their crumpled, white panties. Rose threw up while Lise had an asthma attack during the night and had to be taken to the infirmary, where Coralie

*was already lying on her stomach. A soothing cream, applied by the
gentle Sister Lucy, permitted her to sleep a bit though it was interrupted by convulsive hiccups.*

*For in this hell, there was Sister Lucy. She was a sweet, kind English-
woman from London. She had received a first-rate education and
disapproved of the tortures used on the little girls at the boarding
school. Being severely spanked with a braided, leather whip was
commonplace, but what terrorized the pupils the most was the
dreadful, dark closet where they could be locked up all day on bread
and water. Many a time someone noticed only at bedtime that a little
girl had been forgotten in the dark closet and then went to retrieve
the transgressor who was found asleep, covered with dust, exhausted
from having cried too much, shouted too much, asked forgiveness
too many times, or from being too frightened or wanting to see her
mother or simply die.*

*At the midst of this hell there was Sister Lucy who alone put balm on
the souls of the forty boarders who slept under the eaves, roasting in
summer and freezing in winter. She strolled in the dormitory every
evening dressed in her long, white gown closed up to the neck, her
crossed arms hidden in long sleeves, wearing a small baby-like
bonnet on her shaved hair. She alleviated distress, put her gentle
hand on feverish foreheads, slipped a piece of candy under a pillow,
pulled up a blanket, and disappeared into her cell at the end of the
hall, pretending to forget to put out the kerosene lamp, content to
lower the flame before retiring. Sickened by the incident of the
pantiless, publicly whipped girls, Sister Lucy opened up about it to
her superior, Mother Leonard, asking her to have Miss Yvonne's
brutality stopped. The Mother Superior swore her to silence by
promising to speak to the guilty schoolmistress who continued to be
angry, but who no longer dared resume her public torture sessions.*

*So Coralie grew up this way, loving in all the world only her two
friends, Lise and Rose, and having a distant yet growing adoration for
the gentle, white figure who, like a soothing shadow, passed through
the ominous dormitory every evening and told her quietly with her
strange accent, "Sleep, sleep now, my poor child."*

■   ■   ■   ■   ■

On the tiled walk, a line of little girls moves forward with tiny steps. They are wearing austere, black dresses with white collars. Taut, cotton knit stockings hug their small, easily chilled legs. Each one's hair is parted in the center, and two very tight braids ascend like stiff arches on either side of their small faces numbed by the early morning cold. On their heads float white veils moving like beating wings in the dawn light, their fluttering barely visible on the dim horizon. Attendance is required at mass at dawn whether one is hungry, cold, or still sleepy.

"Coralie, shut up immediately; it's forbidden to speak in line."

"Rose Darcey, don't drag your feet. Lift them up when you walk."

"Lise Alphonsin, straighten your spine. Stand up straight or you'll be hunchbacked."

The little ones bow their small heads beneath the dictatorial voice of Sister Elvire, the headmistress. She is a tall brunette who seems to be a frightening size to the little girls. In her long, brown wool robe with her enormous rosary beads clicking as she walks with big, masculine strides, she resembles a bird of prey, and the wings of her white, winged coif add to this impression. She terrorizes the children in her charge. With her, no prank passes unnoticed. Every fault is severely punished. Her harsh finger immediately points at the offender, and she whacks the child's behind, making her stagger from the blow. She has eyes like ankle-boot buttons that bore to the very core of your soul, and her piercing look extracts halting confessions from the most brazen.

Besides, is it possible to be truly brazen or impudent with Sister Elvire? Like that of a great owl, her shadow hovers over the boarding house whether it be in the classroom, the dormitory or the dining hall. All it takes to begin trembling is to hear the clinking of her rosary beads in the distance and the tapping of her pectoral cross which jolts at each step. She scares all of the pupils to death. In spite of everything, she has her favorites—the tattletales and the sneaks—and Coralie, Rose and Lise are not among them. The three little girls are her victims, and a day doesn't go by without them being harshly beaten. Regularly subjected to the rod, the three friends are only all the more disobedient, more difficult, and Sister Elvire vowed to shape them up at any cost.

That morning after mass, Lise refused to eat the cornmeal porridge, a disgusting gruel swimming with maggots. Sister Agnes, the dining hall prefect, went off immediately to look for Sister Elvire whose arrival was accompanied by the noise of rosary and crucifix.

"Lise Alphonsin, eat your porridge this instant," hissed Sister Elvire to the red-faced little girl, who does not avert her eyes.

"But Sister, there are worms in it," the little girl answers firmly.

"Those worms exist only in your twisted mind," responds Sister Elvire. "Go ahead. Eat!"

The tension increases. Several little girls, among them Coralie Santeuil and Rose Darcey, have placed their tin spoons next to their bowls of gruel. The cowardly snicker and very openly eat their porridge, while several others begin to grumble and mutter.

Sister Elvire sensing the storm coming, must suppress the revolt before it spreads. Why not punish the three ring leaders right away and control the others by threatening similar punishment?

More and more of the little girls put down their spoons. Even those who were eating no longer dare bring to their lips the corn meal porridge beginning to coagulate in the cool bowls.

Sister Elvire, sensing that it is time to get control of the situation before she loses face, orders in a sharp voice, "Everyone, stand up immediately."

Then she takes her rosary and starts a dozen Hail Marys and continues with "Remember, O most blessed Virgin Mary."

The prayer over, she orders, "Everyone, get in line. Go to your classes. Everyone except Coralie, Lise, and Rose, who will stay in the dining hall until they have eaten their entire meal."

Without protest, the girls get up and go out, leaving their three companions, aghast at the outrageousness of the injustice, in front of three bowls of curdled gruel.

"Come on now. Eat that for me at once. You'll stay here all day, and you won't have anything else until you've eaten everything. I have plenty of time."

And Sister Elvire parks herself on a tall chair and calmly begins her rosary.

It is Rose, the gentlest one, who breaks down first. She cries, sobs, and brings a spoonful of the repulsive mixture to her lips. Coralie and Lise continue to keep their heads high, their foreheads smooth, and refuse to open their mouths to eat or beg.

Noon. The little girls come back for lunch. The three condemned ones are in the same place. They take in the aroma of the dishes which have been carefully prepared for the occasion to intensify their suffering.

At the evening meal, they are in the same place, stoic, unbowed. It is only late at night that Sister Elvire, worn down from lack of sleep, finally allows them to stretch out. They carried Rose off a long time ago, slobbering, vomiting, racked by violent hysterics.

For eight days nobody saw Rose, Lise, or Coralie in the boarding school. Locked in the dark closet on bread and water, they eventually came back to their places in class, paler, thinner, but indomitable.

Sister Elvire sent for Coralie's parents, but Aline was the only one to come. She gave permission to the sister to deal even more severely with Coralie, promising her approval of all treatment that might break her stepdaughter's will. But there were no more worms in the morning porridge. And Lise, Cora and Rose were from then on bonded by their shared rebellion.

The insipid life continued, filled with the convent school's unimportant events. There Coralie, indifferent to time's flight, spent sad days. The belts indicating a change of grade level varied at the beginning of each new school year. The Santeuils paid on time, and their daughter succeeded in having the minimum average required for passing to the next grade even though she was at the bottom of the heap.

Coralie watched her friends from the provinces or the capital leaving on Christmas and Easter vacations to join their families who awaited them with excited anticipation. She was the only one who never left the boarding school except for the month of August on summer vacation when Aline, Félicien, and little Marceau went to La Coupe for a short holiday.

Then they took Coralie out of boarding school and, in the cool house in Bois Verna surrounded by tall trees with a shady park in the distance, the little girl at last experienced the fabulous pleasure of being alone. So she stuffed herself with reading and swallowed all of Diloy le chemineau, La Fortune de Gaspard, Les Deux Nigauds, *and the other titles by the Countess of Ségur she was able to find in Marceau's bedroom. Her rather lazy little brother never brought more than one or two volumes of the "Bibliothèque Rose" to keep himself busy during the hot summer at Pétion Ville, yet his bookcase was an inexhaustible treasure for poor Coralie, who stocked up on dreams for the eleven months to come.*

In a hammock under the trees, she sometimes imagined herself as a princess in the tales of A Thousand and One Nights *(the expurgated edition.) A marvelous prince with dark, velvety eyes was going to come to take her away on a tall, white horse to one of Ali Baba's mysterious caves filled with treasure, which he would place at the feet of a bedazzled Coralie blushing beneath her gossamer veil.*

Other days, all of the pent-up energy in her pre-puberty body exploded. On those days, it was the tomboy Coralie who ran wildly in the big garden, galloping, shouting, climbing all the trees, devouring mangoes, guavas, and kenèp, *spotting and tearing her dresses, returning to the big house in the evening in tatters, blades of grass tangled in her hair, her cheeks red from having run too much. Scratched from head to foot by the thorns in the bushes, she felt the wind from her racing and the scratches like a burning mask. She plunged fully dressed into the pool of fresh water in spite of the cries of the servants who shouted, "Ou a pran mal wi Madmwazèl, You're going to get sick, Miss."*

But what did it matter to her if she got sick or not? For a month, Coralie was finally free, free from the boarding school, free from Miss Yvonne, free from Aline. She still detested her stepmother, but she felt a kind of gratitude for being left alone in the big, cool house where August felt so good. Her half-brother, Marceau, was totally indifferent, and her father seemed to be a distant creature constantly wrapped in cigarette smoke, assiduously studying columns of figures, who only showed up to approve of Aline's decisions.

But Augusts have only thirty-one days, and each year the little girl saw the end of this period of celebration approaching all too quickly. Two days after coming down from La Coupe, Aline had Coralie's trunk and the buggy that took her stepdaughter back to the boarding school prepared. The little one received her stepmother's unaffectionate kiss on her forehead and felt Mother Léonard's glance fall on her like an ice tunic. Subjected to this gaze, Coralie felt chilled, and all of the joy of her holiday fell instantly from her skinny shoulders like a garment unsuitable for the austere place to which she had returned.

In September, when the convent was still without boarders, Coralie was practically all alone. Lise and Rose would not return from their provinces, one from Les Cayes, the other from Cap Haitien, until toward the end of the month. Rose would tell effusively about swimming at Camp Perrin. Lise would talk about long walks at Baronnie on her grandfather's land in the northern plains. Radiating gaiety and sunshine, they would glow for endless weeks while Coralie had already felt deadened and wilted for a long time. Waiting for the return of her friends, she would wander through the overly large boarding house taking advantage just the same of the last days when discipline had not yet been strictly reestablished. It is for this reason that Coralie often climbed the low branches of the big mango tree that shaded the covered playground in front of the dining hall. It is from there that she slipped and fell one afternoon.

"Sister Lucy, Sister Lucy. Vini vit, Come quickly," cries the fat, red-haired servant. "Men youn ti madmwazèl sot tonbe nan pye bwa a; li

rete tou rèd, *A young girl has just fallen out of the tree; she's not moving."*

Coralie had a gash on her head and did not regain consciousness until two hours later. The frightened nuns sent for a doctor, but Aline did not consider it necessary to take her stepdaughter back home for such a minor fall, one without serious consequences, according to the doctor. She came to see Coralie twice, lecturing her relentlessly about the unsuitability of climbing trees when you were neither a cat nor a boy, but a big girl who would soon be fourteen years old. Coralie spent two weeks resting, but she suffered from then on from atrocious migraines which attacked her periodically and from which she was never able to fully rid herself.

One morning in the infirmary, she saw her hospital gown spotted with blood. Alarmed, she asked the nurse to call Sister Lucy, and when the gentle nun arrived, Coralie threw herself into her skirts crying and murmuring, "Sister Lucy, Sister Lucy, I'm wounded, wounded inside."

"No, my darling, you aren't wounded … no …."

"Yes, it's from my fall on my head. I broke something inside of me."

"What is happening to you is normal. You are a big girl now. You have become a young lady."

"But the blood …."

"It's what every woman loses each month. It's called menstruation or your period."

So Sister Lucy taught her how to wear pads on these uncomfortable days. From then on, Coralie had another job, that of washing a sack full of stained pads while the older students gathered at the edge of the washhouse stared at her, nudged each other, and shared mocking, little laughs and words filled with mysterious implications.

The hour of the girls' solemn communion arrived, the ceremony with veils, crowns, white dresses decorated with inserts and French lace, *white shoes and fitted stockings. Like her companions, Coralie waited impatiently for this day and followed the ceremonies closely. Surely she too would have a beautiful, organdy dress with beautiful, fluffy decorations, and resemble princesses in fairy tales. Beautiful as a bride, her approach to the Holy Table was to be the marvelous "Open Sesame." The girls would go up to the boarding house to bring flowers to Mary, the Mother of God, and just as soon as the prefect left them, they would hurry to sing:*

It's the month of Mary.

It's the rainy month.

Let's offer an umbrella

to our Blessed Virgin.

It was not a big deal. It was just a pretext to laugh a little because laughter was forbidden during retreats. You were supposed to repress the slightest smile, walk with small, measured steps directly behind the person ahead of you, go to the chapel four or five times daily, sing hymns, hear lots of sermons, and listen to the Gospels. Coralie, her nose in her big missal, notices that Sister Berthe, who reads the Gospel, sometimes skips certain words. Coralie asks herself why. Why not read everything? In her book, it just so happens that she sees in the story of the crucifixion, "Jesus was exposed naked to a large crowd of spectators."

Cora nudges Rose who lowers her face over her book.

"Say, why did she skip 'naked'?"

"I don't know. Leave me alone."

"Why? What's so unusual about being 'naked'?"

"That's enough. Mother Léonard is going to scold us."

"Why?"

"… shush."

The monitor comes to silence Cora authoritatively with her eye and her finger. Later on in the refectory, she will be deprived of her labouyi kè mayi, her cornstarch pudding, and will say a dozen more rosaries than the others for having spoken during retreat. In the evening, Coralie tosses in her bed, tormented by curiosity. "Naked … Why does she always skip naked? Why?"

The disappointment of all of the girls who were to make their solemn communion was atrocious. The Sisters of the Visitation had concocted a horrible communicant's costume which was supposed to save parents money and teach modesty to these young ladies. Imagine a white, cotton dress in the shape of a long shirt over a long-sleeved, pleated smock buttoned down the back, and a skirt hemmed at mid-calf revealing white cotton stockings and low-heeled white shoes. As if this was not scandalous enough, the headdress that crowned the whole thing verged on the ridiculous—a round, shiny straw hat circled with a white, velvet ribbon tied in a bow whose tails hung down the back. Sewn on the ribbon around the brim was a garland of small, white fabric roses badly wobbling on metal wire wrapped with white piping. Never had little girls been more dowdy in approaching the Holy Table, and more than one cried from humiliation and suppressed disappointment. Coralie didn't suffer since she was used to wearing any old thing cut from Aline's cast-off dresses, and Aline found for once that her pupil behaved very well. She kept her eyes dry when other little idiots sobbed uncontrollably.

From the solemn first communion on, it was no longer possible not to go to confession every week on Saturday at three o'clock in preparation for Sunday's mass. And on Sunday morning, they had to fast completely without having eaten or drunk from midnight on in order to approach the Holy Table. The agony of these children, who had supper at six o'clock in the evening and who had to hold out until the next morning at about 8:30 in order to receive communion at High Mass, was unspeakable. More than fourteen hours without eating anything, and especially without drinking, made the divine encounter with the Lord rather bitter. The children blamed themselves for the least bit of swallowed saliva, and it is with dry lips and a parched tongue that they received the consecrated host which would stick without fail to their dry palates. With little, discrete licks, they tried to detach the thin, unleavened wafer without causing too much damage because, above all, their teeth must not encounter the body of Jesus or he would begin to bleed. These beliefs were the source of anguish-filled eyes, contortions of the facial muscles, and eventually of the expression of relief when the sacred Host finally passed, sometimes sideways, into their constricted throats. In the meantime, some of the more nervous little girls burst into tears, while the more clever concealed their efforts behind a face piously hidden in two folded hands.

Coralie was among those who were terrorized at the idea that someday they might bite the body of Jesus, that their mouths would then fill up with an irrepressible flow of blood, and that they would die on the spot and go straight to hell where devils waited to have them roasted for all eternity. So communion days were days of anguish for the poor child, who only came back to life at lunchtime after High Mass when some watery coffee spread a wave of warmth into her heavy chest.

As Coralie approached fifteen, she began to get used to the obliga-tion of going to confession. She had become rather pretty with reddish blond braids and a face sprinkled with freckles. Without being perfectly beautiful, she had the provocative charm of redheads, and her pale, blue eyes had the gentleness of lake waters darkening at times from a gust of wind. She would become beautiful in time when life would endow her thin, angular face with character. Her nervous, whimsical temperament subjected her to mood swings that found her at times the melancholic lover of tall trees and at others the tomboy who still climbed them in spite of the memory of her serious fall.

And then Coralie took a great liking to confession. The boarding school's chaplain had taken a well-earned retirement and had been replaced by Father Rodier, a young priest about thirty years old who, by his masculine presence alone, brought confusion into this house-hold of women of all ages. Tall, but appearing considerably taller, wearing with great elegance his black cassock which showed off his Mediterranean complexion, he rolled his "r's" and sang his "n's" with the touch of an accent that added still more to his charm. But his eyes, oh! his eyes ... velvet, my dear, hazel velvet with golden touches beneath a high, unblemished forehead and a crown of thick, *black hair in a military cut. All of the little girls discovered an appetite for confession. Those who invented important sins were kept longer by the handsome ecclesiastic close to the little door in the confessional that opened and closed with the sound of paradise. Coralie, like the others, was in love with the tall, young man released so imprudently into this aviary. The priest tried to speak Creole which, with his funny accent, was predictably amusing, and the little girls played at imitating their handsome confessor. But unfortunately, the attempts by the young chaplain to understand the Haitian soul were not always successful, and Father Rodier sometimes asked unsuitable questions without realizing the extent of their impact on barely nubile adolescents.*

It is for this reason that he asked Coralie one day, "Eske ou fè move jwèt? Do you play naughty games?"

Goodness, what could that mean? To appear sophisticated, Cora replied with solemnity, "Yes, Father."

That evening, in the dark dormitory, she ran toward Rose's bed.

"Rose, Rose. What does move jwèt mean?

"Leave me alone. I don't know."

"Did Father ask you the same question? Tell me, Rose."

"Yes."

"What did you answer?"

"Confession is a secret."

"If you don't tell me, I'll tickle your feet."

"If you do, I'll laugh and both of us will be caught."

"Dim' non Rose, Tell me, Rose."

"Darn it, I said no."

And Coralie went back to her bed puzzled, wondering if she had been right to answer 'yes' to her confessor's question.

The question recurred each week, and Coralie, caught even more deeply in her own trap, no longer dared revise her first answer. When their paths crossed, the priest often gave her a painful, sad look whose origin she did not understand. She interpreted it as a special interest in her which made her companions jealous. One day, she opened up to Lise Alphonsin. This move jwèt haunted her thoughts now, and she began to fear the unforeseen consequences of her foolish answer. Lise was devastated.

"Cora, what you answered is very bad. Yes, move jwèt means very bad things."

"Like what, for example?"

"Like going to bed with a naked man without being married."

"What? A naked man?"

"Yes, indeed. Or even letting someone touch your private parts, the parts … in short, in your panties. You get it."

"Ooohhhhh!!!"

Horrors! What was the confessor going to think of her? Frightened, Coralie cried all night long. The following Saturday, she pretended she was sick so she did not have to go to confession. Sister Lucy, the dormitory prefect, noticed Coralie's behavior and was questioned by the Mother Superior. Questioned in turn, the priest was driven to say, without breaking the seal of confession, that he had to recognize that this young lady presented a grave danger to the community, that she was perhaps the rotten apple that would spoil the others in the same barrel, and that it would perhaps be best for the good of the entire community to send Coralie home as soon as possible.

Informed of the decision concerning her, Coralie, crushed by shame and injustice, pinched her lips and did not say anything. Sister Léonard promised to pray for her as she was going into the world where she would be exposed to so many more serious temptations than those offered her in the boarding house. But during the night, Coralie had a hideous nightmare: a naked, horned devil ran after her and pushed her into a large hole filled with flames from which she tried to escape. But Aline, who waited for her on the edge of the hole, pushed her back in each time she tried to get out, and the sneering devil had Father Rodier's eyes.

Yelling from terror and soaked with sweat, Coralie woke up with a start and fainted. When she came to, she found Sister Lucy kneeling at the head of her bed softly reciting a prayer. Cora threw herself into her arms. Praying and crying, they remained clasped in each other's arms until dawn, bonded by the sorrow of their imminent separation.

THE SECOND STATION

DECEMBER 31: ARCACHON

7:00 A.M.

On the road that leads from Waney to Carrefour, a poor woman walks painfully. She moves with legs like a pair of wooden stilts, putting one foot forward, catching herself, finding her balance with difficulty, and bringing the other leg back again. She moves very slowly at this pace. It is Coralie Santeuil who is beginning her long quest. First, she will visit Madame Dieufils who lives in Arcachon and who helps her out sometimes. Madame Dieufils is a vendor of *manje kwit*, ready-made food and Coralie is always sure to find a cup of coffee and some biscuits there. This morning, Coralie does not have a cent to her name. She left with a empty stomach and is already famished. Her painful walk brings her to Quénèpe Lane where Madame Dieufils lives. She is panting and recovers her breath a little when she pushes the painted wooded gate enclosing the merchant's modest little garden. But how surprising that on this December 31 morning, Madame Dieufils hasn't opened yet or swept the *devan pòt*, the spot in front of her house. What's going on?

Coralie walks around the little garden and reaches the house's whitewashed back walls shining in the bright daylight.

"E kouzin o … kote ou..? Hey cousin, where are you?"

A door opens half way. It is the shaggy head of Céphise, Madame Dieufils' niece and goddaughter, apparently barely awake.

"Oh, *Ninn' Cora*, auntie Cora, how come you're here so early?"

"I've come to ask my friend for a little coffee."

"I haven't made coffee yet today. My godmother went to Les Cayes three days ago. Our aunt died …."

"E ki lè lap tounin? And when is she coming back?"

"Apre Lèwa wi …. After Epiphany …."

Some residual pride makes Coralie raise her head. She does not dare tell this girl that she has an empty stomach, that hunger has over-taken her, and that, since last evening at about six o'clock, she hasn't eaten anything for lack of money to buy herself even a sweet potato.

"E byen male wi. Na wè endsèjou. Well, good-bye, I'll see you one of these days."

"Mèsi wi. Ma di Nininn mwen ou te pase vini dil bòn ane. Thanks, I'll tell my godmother that you stopped by to wish her a Happy New Year."

Happy New Year, indeed. She stopped by to ask for charity, alms of a cup of coffee and some biscuits. She, Coralie, Félicien Santeuil's only daughter.

So Cora starts out on the road again sorry to have made this addi-tional trip in vain only adding to her weariness and her already great hunger. A sudden gust of wind throws a cloud of dust into her weakened eyes. And tears well up, dry quickly on the back of her rough hand with its broken nails where thick, bluish veins protrude in an arborescent web twisting under her overly delicate skin.

"What dust!"

Her eyes blink and the tears flow.

Dust indeed.

Back there in Madame Dieufils' little house, Céphise splits her sides laughing.

"Sal te ye? What's going on?", asks Wilfred, the young baker who is her current lover, from the bottom of the messy bed.

"Ah, just a lifeless, old lady my godmother would serve coffee to from time to time."

"And why didn't you give her any yourself?"

"*Ou fou?* Are you crazy?", answers the girl, laughing uproariously. "You're crazy, you want her to tell my *ninninn*, my godmother that as soon as she's gone you come to sleep with me? *Ke mwen gen nomm? Ou anraje.* That I have a lover? You're nuts."

With a single movement, she took off the faded shirt she had on when Coralie called. She is a tough, strong griffe, and with an agile leap, she is kneeling on the stomach of the boy whose furry chest hair she pulls in order to excite him. Still laughing, she pecks his mouth with greedy kisses. Then, catlike, she slips in beside him whispering:

"*Kite vye ravèt blanch la al degage li lòt kote non.* Let that old, white-looking cockroach get help somewhere else."

And, like a cat, she slides under the boy who clasps her in his arms and embraces her violently. Later on, Cephise will get up and say to the boy: "*Well now, map fè yon bon ti kafe pou ou,* I'm going to fix you some good coffee," and will add: "*Cheri, ou se nomm dous mwen. Mwen renmen ou anpil. Aswè a tounen bonè tande, map tann ou.* Darling, you're such a wonderful lover .... I love you so much ... Come back very early tonight .... You hear me, I'll be waiting for you."

THREE

Subjected to the shame of her friends' whispers, the nuns' reproachful looks, reinforced by the sighs of the Visitation Convent employees, Coralie, walled in by proud silence, suffered dreadfully. Unable to justify herself to a sympathetic ear, ashamed to show her ignorance and her lack of good judgment, Coralie had to put up with the consequences of a "yes" uttered in a confessional to a priest who was too young and too inexperienced with adolescent psychology. Adolescents, particularly when they lack family affection, have a tendency to create and identify with fictional characters. Coralie was no exception to this general rule, pretending to have committed move jwèt with the sole intention of making herself appear more interesting to the chaplain.

So now, she put up stoically with universal ostracism and dampened her heavy cotton pillow each evening in the dormitory with big, irrepressible, silent tears. She had restless nights and did not fall asleep until dawn, tormented by her increasingly hallucinatory nightmares. Bad nights left her with dark circles under her eyes. Their blueness seemed all the more dazzling contrasted with her purple eyelids from the insomnia that people around her, with elbow jabs and laughter, attributed to her nocturnal "escapades." Then along came the burden of the inquiries to find out who her accomplices were in her alleged vices. Coralie stopped eating, became thinner, and eventually got sick. Once again, they called the doctor. Filled in on the "tendencies" of the poor little girl, he prescribed for Coralie, who scarcely ate anything, besides cold baths and camphor inhalations, a diet less enticing, less rich, less likely to nourish her impulses. From thin, she became skeletal, and her despair, exacerbated by general hostility, forced the nuns to send the "rotten apple" home once and for all.

The day when her stepmother, Aline, pinching her lips in a reproachful pout like somebody picking up a dirty, smelly sock, came to get her, Coralie had her heart broken. She was leaving the boarding house which had been her frequently empty but always comforting *home for seven years and where in spite of everything, she had so long felt secure, protected, appreciated, and sometimes even a little loved. What made her still more sensitive is that in this parlor, where they handed her over once again to Aline's vindictiveness, it was a hired hand, a secretary, who turned her over to her stepmother, who looked at her with the perfect expression of infinite disgust. Sister Lucy didn't even come to embrace her, a final blow to the disconsolate child. The school's doorman carried Coralie's trunk to the family buggy. The young girl, dragging two heavy handbags and a basket herself, followed Aline, who took the lead in this sad procession. Not once did Aline, not even with her fingertips, touch Coralie, who sat with her head bowed, no longer to hold back tears of humiliation.*

Once in the house, Coralie went through hell. Aline created an atmosphere around herself that resembled a safety zone, a moral quarantine, which made the young girl even more of a prisoner than in the convent. She was never permitted to remain alone with her father or any representative of the male sex, be he servant, driver, or gardener. Marceau's mother kept him strictly apart from his older sister, pretending to draw her son close to her the minute Coralie appeared in a room. When Coralie went to Sunday mass with her family, Aline always took great care to put herself between Marceau and Cora so that the children grew up in a climate of suspicion that soon degenerated, thanks to Aline's instigation, into open hate on Marceau's part. Marceau avoided even drinking from a glass earmarked for his sister, who like a leper had her own place settings, chair, sugar, and butter, just as she had her own room and clothing. A clumsy, sneaky servant was assigned to serve the outcast. This disagreeable woman was officially responsible for Cora's bedroom, laundry, and her food, but her secret task was to check to see if she had her monthly periods because "my dear Félicien, one never knows about your daughter's depraved morals."

Félicien Santeuil, weak, apathetic, sickly, and completely dominated by Aline, let her carry on as he deepened the chasm between himself and this child who had reminded him for so long of his first wife. As for Coralie, she did not dare lift her tear-stained eyes towards her beloved father, who from then on was completely ensconced in Aline's camp.

As for her dear boarding school friends, Rose Darcey and Lise Alphonsin, their parents had strictly forbidden them to visit the Santeuils' "lost daughter" because, as one can easily imagine, the reasons for Coralie's dismissal from boarding school had made the rounds of her peers, and the pupils' parents had helped themselves to a good share of the gossip.

If spineless, apathetic, frivolous Rose Darcey had not seen Coralie, the more energetic Lise Alphonsin had done everything to stay in touch with Cora. She had a trustworthy servant deliver Coralie notes in which she made dates for meetings on Sundays in church, at her piano teacher's, or other places, but too deeply wounded to want to explain her conduct to anyone at all, Cora brushed aside Lise's proposals.

Between the ages of sixteen and eighteen, Coralie lived the life of a recluse going out only for Sunday mass flanked by her parents. For other religious services, she endured the supreme torture of being accompanied by Aline alone. When the latter met a friend at the church entrance, she sometimes stopped for a long time to chat without ever introducing her stepdaughter. It was exactly as if Coralie had been transparent, invisible, something like a fugitive phantom floating in Madame Aline Santeuil's wake.

Sixteen years, seventeen years, eighteen years …. Coralie with her delicate, sensitive soul would have suffered martyrdom being in the springtime of life, feeling banished from society, being desperately alone, and condemned to an unfortunate, ambiguous situation if she had not loved reading. While Aline had only a business education, focusing her wily intelligence on increasing the growth of her husband's business, Félicien, on the other hand, was a cultivated man who had good authors in his collection: Flaubert, Balzac, Mériméé, Chateaubriand, Rousseau, and Zola.

So Coralie's imagination, dormant for too long a time, blazed. She was in turn Chateaubriand's Atala and Rousseau's Héloise. She was as frivolous and cynical as Carmen and had an imaginary brother she adored the way Mérimée's Colomba loved Orso. She cried over Madame de Mortsauf's death in Le Lys de la Vallée; she understood and shared Emma Bovary's torments when she wasn't burning beneath her veils like Salammbô. She was Zola's Gervaise and his

Thérèse Raquin, had her bed filled with lovers like Nana, and saved imaginary friends like the generous little prostitute, Boule de Suif. She discovered Anatole France's Thaïs and Pierre Louÿs' Bilitis. She thought she had acquired a great knowledge of love, and what she read in Stendhal did not correct her misconceptions. In short, Coralie Santeuil, on the verge of becoming nineteen, was as ignorant of the things of this world as she was naive about her dreams of happiness. About her beloved books, her companions in her intense solitude, she remembered only the dreamy, fabulous side, and she believed she had lived a lot for having been moved by imaginary adventures and even more for having cried over the tragic misfortune of fictional heroines. Now nineteen, Coralie wanted to contract an interesting pulmonary illness that would cause her death and her redemption by love like Marguerite Gauthier, la Dame aux Camélias, in the arms of an ardent, repentant lover.

Completely absorbed by her extraordinary, imaginary adventures, Coralie did not notice right away that the atmosphere around her was changing imperceptibly. To begin with, Aline, who dressed her stepdaughter dowdily in her old, altered dresses in order to do her best to cover Cora's thin body, got it into her head that the young girl needed a more adequate wardrobe. She took Cora to her dress-maker, had some fashionable dresses made for her, bought her several pairs of French shoes at Paul Auxila's boutique, taught her how to use makeup sparingly and to perfume herself even more discretely, to raise her head, and to learn how to smile again.

Now when Aline met her friends after mass or vespers, she intro-duced Coralie graciously. At first she said "my stepdaughter, Cor-alie," then "my husband's daughter" followed by "Félicien's eldest child," and Coralie thought she would die from a seizure one day when Aline introduced her to three astonished ladies by saying "my daughter" with the most gracious smile on her lips ordinarily puck-ered in a scornful sneer.

Coralie, who had become beautiful and elegant, thought she was living in a fairy tale much more marvelous than the novels that ordinarily nourished her. Certainly it was her father who must have ordered his wife to treat his daughter better, dress her suitably, and introduce her to society. When she looked in her dressing-table mirror, she saw the image of a pretty girl with a slender neck, a pale pink, perfectly oval face framed by heavy, reddish blond braids and brightened by a pair of periwinkle-blue eyes, that were at once gentle, lively, thoughtful, and guileless. Resembling a Saxon porcelain, a Tanagra, this Coralie's coral lips murmured ever so nicely a prayer to the god of lovers that he send her a prince charming soon.

While waiting, Aline opened her door to some high society women who brought along their daughters and sons to the modest but select receptions Madame Santeuil gave to introduce "her daughter." Events went along in this fashion for about a year. Then one day, quite suddenly, the light dawned in Coralie's mind. Aline hoped quite simply to marry her off. All of these expenses, clothes, outings, and receptions were designed solely to get rid of her, to chase her from her father's house once again, to find another home for her once and for all so as not to have the annoyance of her presence and the expense of her upkeep anymore.

Cora, naive and good, had sincerely believed that her stepmother, even though coerced in her view by Félicien, had reverted to more human feelings towards her. Cora locked herself up in her bedroom for three days, cried a lot, and did not eat. She was going to punish Aline for her hypocrisy. She was going to return to all her old rags, not comb her hair, not put on makeup, and refuse to shake hands or smile at Aline's friends. She was going to ... in her view, she was going to punish her stepmother by taking away from her the advantage of parading her around like an animal exhibited at a fair in order to be sold.

But the heart of a twenty-year old needs to be out in the open. A girl of twenty likes to feel pretty and well dressed, a twenty-year old's stomach needs nourishment, and Coralie had adopted habits shaped by luxury and abundance. And this admiration for her beauty that she read in everyone's eyes had become as necessary to her as breathing.

At the end of three days of pouting during which she refused to speak to Aline and Félicien who had knocked at her door several times, Coralie came down to the dining room made up, coiffed, and wearing a pretty blue dress which showed off to advantage her shining eyes. Aline knew that she had won and, for once, did not gloat contenting herself with tossing out a "Are you feeling better, my dear?" filled with hypocritical solicitude.

It is this resigned, crushed Coralie who, having crucified her dreams in the depths of her eyes, agreed three months later to wed Gratien Nivel, a very prosperous businessman. He was almost the age of her father, Félicien, shorter than his future wife by at least a head, chubby, short-legged, potbellied, and bald to boot. During her short engagement, Coralie was giddy from the flood of gifts received from her future husband. On her left ring finger sparkled an enormous sapphire surrounded by twenty tiny blue-white diamonds that Nivel had given her as an engagement ring. Every day she received an abundance of presents, flowers, candies, perfumes. Gratien, who had been a widower for more than twenty years, was dazzled by his fiancée's beauty, and without realizing it, she found herself enjoying being flattered, spoiled, deified. When Gratien raised himself up to touch Coralie's lips, she closed her eyes and let him do it. In her heart of hearts, she truly hoped that on the wedding day, a fairy with the touch of a magic wand would come to transform her old toad of a husband into the dazzling prince charming of her dreams.

THE THIRD STATION

DECEMBER 31: MAHOTIÈRE

8:00 A.M.

Coralie moves shakily along Carrefour's main road. Hunger gnaws at her stomach, and she suddenly thinks about her old friend Onésime Defossé, called Zizim, who will not refuse her a breakfast. Provided that Zizim is at his counter. He will surely accommodate her just as he had already done in the past. But in order to go to Thor where Zizim runs a successful brothel, she must cross the main road, and it is always a drama for Coralie whose unsure legs do not enable her to slip between the *tap-taps*. She almost gets run over twice while crossing the street, and the van with the inscription "Dieu plus Fort" (God the Strongest) practically throws her into the gutter. Breathless, she leans on the road sign and starts walking toward the "Foufoune Bar," sticking close to the shoulders, paying careful attention to the stones that roll under her clumsy feet.

Onésime sits enthroned in a rocking chair in front of his door. The morning is his time to relax, his moment of rest. The "Foufoune Bar" only comes to life at nightfall and, at this hour, the six or seven girls who make up his "herd" are sleeping with the exception of Ramona, who is washing two inexpensive, black lace bras in the establishment's courtyard. She is the first one to see the visitor.

"*Qué tal, Mama Cora?*", "What's happening, Mama Cora?, she utters with her throaty laugh.

"Just fine, my dear, thanks. And happy New Year to you."

"Happy New Year," responds in Spanish the girl who goes inside rolling her buttocks and humming a Dominican tune.

Onésime turns his head toward Coralie who moves jerkily forward. His morning snooze has just been interrupted, and he gets ready to chase away the intruder who has the audacity to come along and keep him from recuperating his hours of lost sleep. But when he sees Coralie, his fat, broad face breaks into a fine, kind-hearted smile revealing his toothless gums. His moist lips stretch out into a kind of palatalized hiss.

"Cora chè, ala bòzò ou bòzò maten an. Ou santi joudlan an? Sak pase? Cora, my dear, you're really dressed up this morning. You're in the spirit of the New Year? What's up?"

"Adye Zizim, anyen pa bon. Lwaye kay mwen bout, map pran lari poum chèche kote ma jwen lajan sila a. Se pa fasil. Alas, Zizim, things are not going well. I don't have any money for the rent. I'm out looking for where I can find it. It's not easy."

At the word *lajan*, money, Onésime's face clouds over. He likes Cora well enough to give her small gifts, but it is a long way from that to lending her a big sum of money to pay her rent. He knows that she is penniless, and Onésime never makes bad business deals. After a silence, he says in a slow voice, "This week things are not going well at all. Things are really tough."

"Mwen kon sa. Mwen pa vini mande ou prete. I know that. I haven't come here to ask you to lend me money. I have two or three people to see in Port-au-Prince. I'll see what they can do for me. I just would like some coffee from you."

Onésime's plump belly expands still more in his bold, red sweater which hugs two fat, flabby nipples. He smiles from relief, and his small eyes disappear in his moon-shaped face. His tight, yellow skin seems to become still lighter. He lifts his Asiatic, pot-bellied body out of his rocking chair and calls with a suddenly more lively voice:

"Estina, vini vit. Fri de zeu pou Ninn' Cora. Mete youn bon ti aransò ak bannann bouyi kote l epi pote l vini. Estina, come here. Fry two eggs for Aunty Cora. Add some good smoked herring with two boiled plantains, and then bring the meal here. Get some fresh bread, and after you've done that, serve her some good, hot coffee *pou kore l*, to give her strength...."

Getting up laboriously out of his rocking chair, Onésime takes Coralie by the hand and guides her into the room where most of the chairs are perched on the tables. A nonchalant waiter pushes a listless mop on the floor sprinkled with wood shavings.

"Alò, Coralie,*ou pral wè mesye ou yo,* you're going to see your boys?"

"What else do you expect me to do, Zizim? *Se yo sèl mwen genyen.* They're all I've got."

"That's true. You couldn't do anything else."

The steaming breakfast arrives carried by Estina, the cook. Coralie is already salivating. She controls herself, calmly breaks the bread, and begins to eat her eggs with an elegant slowness that makes Onésime's toad-like paunch shake as he snickers, *"A la fanm konn manje bwòdè! Ou gen rezon di lè ou te piti ou te gwo moun.* This woman really eats elegantly! You are right when you said that you grew up with style among the elite."

Poor Cora, who was upset with herself for having kept such distinguished manners in her misery, almost lost her appetite because of the proprietor's remark.

"Ledikasyon, se bèl bagay, san repròch. Good manners are a beautiful thing, aren't they?", continues Zizim, not realizing that he is hurting his guest's feelings.

Coralie hurries to finish the substantial breakfast and hastily swallows her coffee, burning her lips.

"Bon map fè panyòl wi, map demake tou swit paske rout mwen long jodi a e mwen pa gen kòb pou m pran kamionèt. Well, I'm taking off. I've got to leave right now because I have a long way to go, and I don't have any money for a taxi."

The proprietor becomes somber instantly. It is easy to offer a meal, but giving up the smallest coin gives him a stomach ache.

"*Mwen swete ou bòn rout.* I wish you a good journey", he says, slapping her on her raised shoulder, practically making her hunch over.

"*Mèsi anpil,* Zizim, thanks a lot, Zizim, thanks. *Bondye va remèt sa ou fè maten an.* The Good Lord will reward you for what you did this morning."

From the side of the road, Cora looks at the asphalt ribbon that unfolds in front of her. She still has a long way to walk. Her frightened eyes see the rainbow colored, beribboned *tap tap.* Tomorrow is New Year's Day and some vans have attached bunches of multi-colored balloons to their rear-view mirrors. And they go by quickly, crammed with passengers, their radios blaring holiday music, their axles practically dragging on the ground from the human cargo weighing them down. These *tap tap,* these jitneys are going so fast! "Vive Perpetuel" (Long live Our Lady of Perpetual Help), "Merci l'Eternel" (Thanks, Eternal One), "Saint Sauveur" (Holy Savior) ... Saint Sylvester, can you do something for Coralie, December's passer-by?

FOUR

The marriage of Coralie Santeuil and Gratien Nivel was the big event of the Port-au-Prince social season. A mild, cool month of December, not unheard of in Haiti, a cold sky studded with twinkling stars, and a clear, pure night allowed the Santeuils to have a grandiose reception out of doors. All of the garden's tall trees were decorated with lights, and the shrubs, tied with white and pink ribbons, quivered in the breeze. Large, silver paper bandoleers linked the arbors and pergolas. A successful wedding, a superb reception, all the more so because it was Nivel, twenty times richer than the Santeuils, who paid the bills. Everyone knew that Aline would never have incurred this crazy expenditure, but because traditionally it is the parents of the bride who entertain the guests, Aline, decked out in salmon lace, took great pleasure in playing the role of the attentive hostess without opening her pocketbook.

As ridiculous as Gratien Nivel was, stuffed into pearl gray tails and striped pants, people forgot the disparity in age, size, and demeanor when they saw the bride alone, going from group to group, surrounded by the joyful swarm of her bridesmaids shepherded by Rose Darcey and Lise Alphonsin who, besides being in the wedding procession, had been Coralie's witnesses.

Félicien Santeuil had escorted his daughter to the altar on the arm of one of Gratien Nivel's sisters-in-law. Nivel had done his very best to get the others to understand that a widower of his age, without a wife for twenty years, that is to say since the time of Coralie's birth, already elderly and not particularly handsome and elegant, owed it to himself to have a discreet remarriage, especially when he was marrying a young woman. Aline had made sparks fly and shouted loudly. What? But a girl only gets married once in a lifetime with "veil and crown" in a church, and "their" daughter was a true young lady brought up carefully in the convent, practically cloistered by her devoted parents, never tainted with any "messing around," so life owed her the beautiful wedding that any devoted, loving mother could wish for her. In short, Nivel was forced to subject himself to

Aline's onslaughts and to consent to the most unreasonable expenses for the engagement, trousseau, house, furniture, silverware, the ceremony at Sacred Heart of Jesus, and the grandiose reception, not to mention the honeymoon in Kenscoff's best hotel.

Nivel had consented to everything. Impressed by his young fiancee's beauty, her model's body, and her grace and natural elegance, but mostly because she sometimes deigned to place a simultaneously tender and playful kiss on the top of his bald head, he promised himself to make happy this exceedingly young and pretty wife who had agreed to embellish his life, the old, stammering gnome as rich as he was ugly, as lonely as he was rich.

A speculator in and exporter of coffee, Nivel had not had any children from his first wife. With a temperament made more reserved due to his physical ugliness, he withdrew into solitude, resigning himself to a sad old age. It just so happened that, having entered the Santeuils' store by chance to pick up several bottles of aged Bordeaux, he had noticed this Sylph with azure eyes and liquid gold hair. He had inquired discreetly about her from a salesman and had learned that this superb, exceptionally tall, slender girl was the owner's daughter. And that very evening, he had his sister-in-law, the wife of his younger brother who did business with Félicien, introduce him to the Santeuils.

Nivel, who wasn't lacking finesse, very quickly realized that, first of all, it was Aline who wore the pants in the Santeuil household and that it was of prime importance to gain her good graces, and second, that the good graces of Madame Santeuil would not be difficult to obtain, for Aline wanted above all else to get rid of her step-daughter. Coralie, defeated, resigned, and anxious as well to escape Aline's hold without delay, had let the latter take affairs in hand, worrying little about how she would finally leave her parents' dwelling. Aline, who felt that Nivel was hooked like a fish and madly in love with Coralie, had pushed the dear man quite far. She had asked and obtained for Coralie a pretty villa located between a courtyard and a garden at Pacot, a deluxe car with a chauffeur, a case filled with beautiful jewels, a queen's trousseau, and dishes and silverware from the best manufacturers, not to mention the bride's dress, the grandiose ceremony with a chorale, and the sumptuous reception, the crowning achievement of her competence as a marriage broker. Coralie would be truly ungrateful if she did not appreciate the fabulous marriage that Aline had negotiated for her. One never knew with such a strange daughter who locked herself up for an entire day in her room to cry. Aline, whose only true God had always been money, had married Félicien only in hopes of taking over this business in which her father was the first employee, did not understand that, with the fortune that she was going to inherit sooner or later, Coralie would not be thoroughly happy. She did not understand why the young girl would sigh occasionally at great length while her china blue eyes watched the setting sun plunge into the bay of Port-au-Prince or when playing a Chopin nocturne. Fi sa dwol vre! This girl is really strange! thought Aline when saying good-bye to the Santeuils' and the Nivels' last guests.

Then it was eventually time to leave for the honeymoon. What a dream! An anticipated week at Villeflor in the best room and in an idyllic natural setting. And Aline made sure that the two small trunks of the wedded couple's clothing were in the Duisenberg's back trunk stocked with a basket of snacks so that the wedded couple would be sure to have food available on their wedding night.

"Cover up well, my dear," Aline says to Coralie who was shivering in the December night. "It's going to be very, very cold. Here, take this shawl ...."

"Let me take care of it, dear Aline," interrupts Nivel, signaling the driver to lift a large, beribboned box from the back seat from which Nivel took out a white, ermine cape with which he covered his young wife's quivering shoulders and to whom he whispered tenderly:

"Thank you for all of the happiness that you give me. Thank you for letting me spoil you."

"It's I who ...," begins Coralie, but words fail her, and it is with a lump in her throat that she leans her cheek toward Nivel, uttering faintly:

"You are good, so good, thank you."

She promised herself to do everything to bring happiness to this generous man who had saved her from the vise in which she had been squeezed in Aline Santeuil's house.

The car left at top speed for Pétion-Ville, then Kenscoff, and during the whole trip, Gratien held his wife's left hand where a wedding ring fashioned from a row of small diamonds had just joined the engagement sapphire.

■ ■ ■ ■ ■

In their room adjoining a small, private drawing room, Gratien Nivel helped his young wife to undress, the back of her satin and lace dress having been closed with thirty tiny pearl buttons held in place by fasteners. When the dress fell around Coralie like petals from a flower, she appeared in elated Gratien's eyes like a tall lily in her fluffy, snow-white undergarments.

Touched, embarrassed, he cleared his throat and said with an unexpectedly hoarse voice:

"I … I'm going to get ready in the bathroom. You … you can make yourself comfortable … I … I'm coming back."

And he disappeared into the bathroom where Coralie heard him performing several ablutions. She continued to get undressed, took off her shoes and stockings, kept on her white lace panties, and slipped into a superb white linen nightgown with embroidery on tulle executed by Marie Madeleine's nimble-fingered girls.

With a sigh, she got into the chilly bed that no one had thought about warming up with a bed warmer. She pulled the blanket up under her chin and put out one of the two lamps placed on her side of the bed.

Then she waited. Not very long because she soon heard Gratien turn off the electric light switch in the bathroom. And there he was all round and all pink moving into the bedroom in a pair of silk pajamas trimmed with navy blue and a matching pocket handkerchief in the same color. A whiff of Caron's cologne "Pour un homme" invaded the room where Coralie, paralyzed with astonishment, huddled at the bottom of the big, brass bed. In her whole life, Coralie had never seen a man in intimate apparel, not even her father, who was always properly dressed at home just as he was at work.

And Gratien moved forward with a strange expression on his face. Good gracious, how he had changed; he seemed older, his features more set. Suddenly Gratien smiled, and Coralie understood.

His teeth! He had left his teeth in the bathroom and was moving toward her with a big, shadowy hole between his nose and his chin.

And suddenly, from the depths of her being, her irrepressible laughter burst out, striking Nivel right in the face. The uncontrollable laughter unfurled itself, filled up the room, rolled onto the bed, and clung to the curtains, like an angry torrent of water that rushes down a mountain, water with which Coralie was now soaked, for the laugher broke into convulsive sobs that she could not repress, just like the trills that had filled her throat shortly before.

Gratien put out the lights and, with infinitely slow movements, slipped in beside Coralie, who by now was crying with short, gasping sobs. In the dark, he held her hand until, exhausted from tears and distress, she finally fell asleep in the wee hours of the morning. Then he got up quietly and went to stretch out noiselessly on the sofa in the little drawing room where a heavy sleep eventually came to deliver him from his cruel deception.

It was only on the last night of their stay at Kenscoff that, touched by the goodness, patience, and gentleness of her husband, Coralie finally consented to a pitiful embrace between her troubled, humiliated husband and her disappointed, frustrated self.

Once they had settled into their villa at Pacot, the Nivels tacitly consented to separate bedrooms. Nivel used as a pretext his habit of *working late and rising early in order to let Coralie have complete possession of the master bedroom and the large, empty bed where each night the phantom of a young, handsome prince charming, dressed in silk from head to foot and who smiled at her with a toothless mouth, came to visit her.*

THE FOURTH STATION

DECEMBER 31: THOR

9:00 A.M.

Fortified by the substantial breakfast given to her by Zizim, the brothel's proprietor, Coralie feels a little stronger. But her purse remains just as empty, and she needs to find a few cents, some *gourdes* to make the trip toward Port-au-Prince, not to mention the distance she must cover to see her sons, one living in Bois Verna and the other in Musseau. She thinks about Mathias Casal, the *Mèt Jwa*, the Game Master, who has often helped her out in the past. He has his gambling joint several yards from the spot where Carrefour's old road joins the new one, and Cora, cheered up by a good meal, now feels strong enough to make this rather long trip.

She pushes open the door decorated with a distasteful sculpture. The hinges creak without attracting the attention of the place's occupants. At this early-morning hour, the night's smoke has not vanished yet, and the air is thick enough to cut with a knife. Coralie's eyes blink, and she holds back involuntary tears. At the same time, the intoxicating odor of wood shavings mixed with kerosene and spread on the tiled floor clings to her throat. A toothless boy stinking of rum pushes this slippery mixture with a broom wrapped in a filthy rag between the legs of the gamblers who could not care less.

The clicking of the polished ivory chips alternates with the clacking of the dominoes moved cautiously by three men seated at a table, one of whom is already wearing, at ten o'clock in the morning, an antique metal lamp shade on his head which formerly served to protect the bulb of an old Electric Company street lamp.

At a table, four men playing a game called "bézigue" are thinking about the most astute way to turn up a matching king and queen for forty points or four aces for a hundred points while openly eyeing a pile of dirty cards softened by sweaty hands. And Cora wonders how the skinniest of the players, a clothespin pinching his nose, manages to continue breathing.

"*Bwa nan nen, bwa nan nen,* You've got a pin on your nose, you've got a pin on your nose," sneer his partners.

And all of the gamblers in this pitiful little group are already sweating profusely in spite of the early-morning hour. Enclosed by colored windows, the room contributes to the perspiration on their foreheads which are wrinkled from concentration and the anxiety of losing. How can they gamble away everything, losing the precious few *gourdes* they earned behind the wheel of a *tap tap* or by stretching out under a motor dripping dirty oil, screwing or unscrewing nuts, or shouting in the streets "*Men gwo lo a wi,* I am selling the winning number!" How can they risk their daily earnings by coming here to lose it in this hovel, hoping to triple their slim, daily profit under the expressionless eye of the Game Master—the only one to grow richer from their misery?

At the bar, a dreamy girl chases some flies off the shiny Formica top which is chipped where the metal rim has given way. Haloed by pink and green curlers, she seems to have descended from a painting by Saint Soleil, the bright, blue dress hugging her generous breasts which she bobs indifferently under the noses of the clients. From time to time, she brings them a glass of alcohol on a sticky tray, ordered from afar by a signal which means "the same thing."

How many of "the same thing" have they drunk since midnight last night? And this December 31 day, they have all decided to cop out, counting on gambling to bring into their poor homes the provisions for New Year's Day: the promised New Year's gifts, the dress or the new shoes, if not the miracle medication. What good does it do to work one more day in this bitch of a year if one lucky throw of the dice can save everything? And they continue to play, slaves of this false pleasure, heedless of Cora's distress so like their own.

Coralie Santeuil passes through the thick smoke to the bar where she props up her long, lopsided silhouette. The waitress looks at her menacingly:

"*Bonjou Rosana, Kote Mathias,* Good morning, Rosana. Where is Mathias?"

"*B'jou. Li dèyè a wi.* Good day. He's back there."

"*Eske mwen mèt wè li?* Can I see him?"

"*Ou met antre. Degaje ou.* Come on in. Make yourself at home."

Is there some malice in this last sentence? An evil glimmer lights up her dull glance for an instant. With her chin, Rosana motions to Coralie to advance into the nook that serves as Mathias Casal's office and bachelor's quarters. Fearlessly, Coral pushes open the door with one of those abrupt movements caused by her infirmity and stops at the threshold of the room. Disturbed in one of his revels with a barely pubescent girl, the *Mèt Jwa*, gets up, adjusts his disheveled clothing, and says to the sad looking little girl:

"*Rale cò ou! Ale vou zan!* Get out of here! Go away!"

Coralie, shaking, doesn't dare move forward or backward. The brute resumes with a sneer:

"*Fok ou nonm pran yon ti anmizman tanzantan.* A man has to have a little fun from time to time."

Then he adds:

"*Ki bon van ki mennen ou maten an?* Look what the wind blew in! What do you want, Cora? What are you doing here?"

On the verge of tears, the disconcerted woman stammers:

"*Mwen gen ou ti kòb poum touche maten an, men mwen pa gen kòb kamyonèt pou mal kote moun ki pou peyem nan.* I have to go get some money this morning, but I don't have any money for transportation so I can get to the person who is going to give it to me."

Mathias smiles in a seemingly cunning way.

"Cora, don't beat around the bush. *Dim ou razè se tout!* Just tell me you're broke."

Without answering, Coralie bows her head so that the slovenly man in front of her won't see the flash of disgust that lights up her emotionless eyes.

"Follow me. I'll give you a little bit of money. When your hand touches mine, it brings me luck."

He has helped Coralie more than once. Extremely superstitious, he has supposedly observed that the days Coralie taps him for a little money are the lucky days when the greenhorns in his gambling joint are even more royally fleeced.

He moves into the room where the gamblers continue to *téquer,* maneuver the chips and calls Rosana twice.

From the small, back courtyard come shrill yells. It is Rosana "who is whipping" her little sister.

"*Vèmin, bouzen, se sa ou vin fe Potoprens?* You good for nothing, you whore. Is this what you came to Port-au-Prince to do? Is this what your mama sent you here for? *Gade rizèz la non.* Look at you, you little sneak. Didn't I forbid you to go into the owner's room? *Gade lè ou non, je chèch, manman epav!* Look at you, standing here pretending that nothing happened. You have no shame, you little slut!"

The abuses fall with increasingly heavy blows on the little girl, who howls at the top of her lungs.

Mathias shouts:

"*Tonnerre! Sispann mwen sa. Rosana, ki dwa ou pou bat ti fi a?* God damn it! Stop it. Rosana, who gives you the right to beat her?"

The perspiring sister enters and throws Mathias a furious look. She gasps:

"*Se pa jenès manmanm te voye l fè nan Pòtoprens.* My mom didn't send her to Port-au-Prince to be a prostitute. This was not the reason you told me to have her come from our village."

Rosana, her curlers hanging pitifully around her swollen face, now cries bitterly.

Mathias Casal bangs his fist on the formica. Two glasses half-full of liquid and flies knock against one another and tip over.

"*Pe la, pe dan ou mwen di ou. Si l te bon pou ou, li ka bon pou li tou. Sak te gen tan gen la a?* Shut up, I told you to shut up. If it was good for you, it could be good for her, too. What's the big deal? Who do you think you are? When you take my money to send to your mother, the money doesn't smell bad to her. *Lajan an dous pa vre? Alò fok tout lòt bagay dous tou.* The money is good, isn't it? So anything else has to be good, too. Do you understand what I mean? *Sispann eskandal sa a tou swit ban mwen.* Stop the scandal right away."

Defeated, Rosana sniffles and dries her tears with the back of her hand. Mathias puffs up like a peacock and says in a way that everyone around him can hear:

"Fifty *gourdes*. Ten dollars. It's for Coralie. Fifty gourdes!"

Much more than enough for some taxi rides, it is a week of steady meals, it is freedom from this hunger that is her constant companion. Yet, for a second, she wants to refuse. The scene of the man seducing the little girl comes back to her. She wants to refuse, but her eager body protests. To eat her fill for four or five days … She extends a trembling hand. A painful "thanks" comes out of her contracted throat. Then she thinks that she doesn't have the means to cut herself off from the generosity of the *Mèt Jwa*, the Game Master, and faintly adds, "Happy New Year."

Shaking and staggering, she quickly crosses the threshold of the smoke-filled hovel where the gamblers have paid scant attention to a rather commonplace scene.

Close to the gate, Rosana's little sister continues her sobbing. Her *caraco* is torn where her big sister's blows have pulled off her delicate skin along with bits of the faded fabric that is far too thin for this December morning. In some spots, the blood is already coagulating. The dress sticks to the blood-tinged scars given to her by her sister and rival for the master's favor.

Coralie holds the chin of the little one who makes hiccuping sounds, her eyes flooded with tears, her limpid glance going straight to her heart. The ten dollar bill passes from Coralie's long, skinny hand into the tear-drenched one of the little girl, and the poor woman surprises herself by saying to the woe-begone child:

"Men, rantre lakay ou pitit mwen. Ale, pa rete isit la; tounen jwenn manman ou. Men pou pran okazyon. Here, take this. Go home now, my little one. Go away, don't stay here; go back to your mom. Take this to pay for the bus fare."

The child looks at Coralie with a stunned expression, then at the money, then once again at the woman who is stroking her hair. Then she takes off like a young goat towards the southern highway.

■ ■ ■ ■ ■

Cora wastes no time in resuming her long walk toward the capital.

FIVE

A modus vivendi, simple in appearance but in reality extremely complex, established itself smoothly in the life of Coralie and Gratien.

The Nivel couple presented an unruffled, calm facade to the world. The plan was uncomplicated: the older husband adored his young wife and spoiled her like a Santa Claus whose presents appeared daily. In exchange, Coralie brought Gratien the comfort of her youthful presence, her happy, girlish laughter, her more filial than conjugal tenderness. They had a very intense social life, and everywhere they went, they were full of attention for one another. Nivel willingly carried Coralie's scarf and her small, sparkling, beaded bag or he would dine at a table with some friends while his young wife whirled in the arms of an intrepid waltzer. After the dance, when she came back to their table breathless and flushed with pleasure, escorted by a handsome dancer, the husband inquired with a pleasant smile:

"You're not too tired, my darling?"

"Not at all. I'm just very thirsty."

"Don't budge. I'll bring you a glass of champagne."

"Thanks, Gratien. You spoil me too much."

Beautiful, elegant, rich, Coralie Nivel, in spite of her extreme youthfulness and the pressing compliments of a court of admirers, remained beyond reproach. At receptions, people saw her hurrying to prepare the plate that she never failed to first provide for her husband, choosing his favorite dishes, avoiding the sugar harmful to his diabetes, or adding a sweetener, which she always carried in her handbag, to his coffee.

This picture of a tender, conjugal happiness was idyllic in appearance only. On certain evenings, the pretty Madame Nivel suddenly laughed too loudly at some rather salacious jokes whispered in the hollow of her pearl-studded ears by a bolder partner. She sometimes took imprudent walks in the shadowy groves beneath some accommodating moonlight, and more than one hand attempted to explore her bosom, more than one face approached hers to kiss her lightly on her perfumed temples, and she occasionally experienced a sudden warmth that rushed through her veins and made her throbbing breasts blush. Coralie became very flirtatious when playing this game, and it became rather quickly known that Madame Nivel was a flirt who promised a lot, who permitted some undue familiarities, but who was entirely faithful to her husband who followed her everywhere, at least during the early months.

Gratien soon returned to his exports, balance-sheets, concern about the falling price of coffee, the decrease in production, and the competition from Brazilian and Colombian coffees. He came home late from the office, tired from his work, constantly concerned about his diabetes that demanded monitoring, and the mundane life, becoming more and more unpleasant to endure, that his young wife had forced him to lead.

So the aged husband gradually acquired the habit of letting Coralie go out alone. At first, friends came by to pick her up and bring her back. Sometimes Gratien asked the chauffeur, Marcel, a strapping young man, to accompany Coralie on her nocturnal outings. This boy, apparently from a good family, had excellent manners, and only a reversal of fortunes had forced him to accept a job as a private driver. From better days, he had retained a distinguished bearing that Coralie's friends noticed with pleasure. He was very flattered to escort his pretty employer.

"Your driver is very handsome, Coralie. And what class!"

"He wears the uniform elegantly; he seems very well bred."

"In short, it's John, the prince and chauffeur, in person," teased Coralie's friends, Lise Alphonsin and Rose Darcey, with whom she had renewed a warm, close relationship.

They told one another about their memories of boarding school, stories known by them alone, which made them burst out laughing in their private conversations. Moreover, Madame Gratien Nivel was Port-au-Prince's darling. She was at all of the balls, all of parties at the Sea Side Inn, the Parisiana, La Rivière Froide. Her fortune, flaunted in dresses, jewels, and cars, brought her a multitude of new acquaintances who envied her and slandered her, all the while trying to imitate her boyish haircut, long, mother-of-pearl cigarette holder, very low-cut pastel dresses, and Paul Poiret suits. Her favorite perfumes were Guerlain's "Shalimar" for the daytime and Jean Patou's "Joy" for evening, so all elegant women begged their husbands for them. And it was she who launched a stunning fragrance, Schiaparelli's "Shocking," a perfume well known as an aphrodisiac, which became the elegant, female city dwellers' great extravagance.

This life of a frivolous butterfly concealed a deep moral distress. Coralie's nights were nothing but a long search for a restless sleep. The words whispered in her ear, the compliments about her beauty excited her greatly and the gentle caresses she permitted awakened a thousand unfulfilled desires.

She often spent her night in tears, and if she got up late, it was not only to avoid the morning kiss of an ever more wrinkled Gratien, but also to hide from her keenly observant husband her eyes, encircled from crying and swollen from the feverish expectation of impossible happiness.

Poor Gratien Nivel became more gentle and more attentive on those days when Coralie, nervous and irritable, bullied the servants, shouted for no apparent reason, smashed a precious vase to calm her nerves, and eventually broke into convulsive sobs for next to nothing.

These angry outbursts occurred especially after a visit from the Santeuils, who lunched twice monthly in the home of their son-in-law and daughter and stepdaughter at a dull meal at which Coralie imitated the perfect happiness of the blissful wife attentive to the needs of her adored husband. After the Santeuils' departure, Coralie, overcome by migraine headaches, had another of her fits of hysterics which occasionally caused her to faint. Desperate, the kind Gratien did everything to calm her. He coaxed her, rocked her, yet Coralie sometimes repelled angrily, almost with rage, the approaches of her *frustrated, disappointed husband, who was even more disturbed than she by what he understood about her afflictions. Sometimes she repulsed him harshly, and he remained on his knees on the living room carpet while she ran off to lock herself in her bedroom, where he heard her pacing angrily until late into the night.*

It was worse on other evenings. Having learned to drive with the handsome Marcel, she now got along without his services after nightfall. Alone, when her migraines were the most acute, she spent hours driving at full speed or stopping at a bar to have a drink with strangers. The moment the latter became audacious and vulgar, she took off into the night, driving at a deadly pace, not coming home until dawn to throw herself on her bed and sleep until noon with a deep, dreamless sleep.

And what was destined to happen, happened: a first intimate relationship with a handsome French navy officer passing through whom she had met while visiting the "Joan of Arc" lying at anchor in the bay. The visit of the ship had impressed her, and the handsome officer turned guide had fallen in love with this splendid, red-haired creature who had such beautiful teeth and a model's body.

Later, after copious glasses of Dom Perignon, when he had possessed her in his quarters, he had been surprised to find her virtually virgo intacta, and he had regretted having been the first to initiate this young woman who had appeared so sexually experienced.

From her one and only night with the handsome captain, Coralie had remembered only the intoxication from the champagne and the violent pain that had torn her body. She remained unsatisfied until the day when the secretary from the Dominican embassy managed to arrange a meeting with her. It just so happened that Coralie had never held in her arms the body of a young, vigorous man at the height of his manliness. Expert in love games, the young Panyòl, this Latin-American man, introduced her to the most ardent sensual pleasures. She saw this man, who captivated her repeatedly, until the day when, to her great dread, she perceived that she truly, totally loved him and that she wanted to join her life to his forever. Yes, she was going to accompany Mario to the Dominican Republic, marry him, bear him children, and follow him to the ends of the earth on all of his assignments. One evening, she decided to tell Gratien. He was good, he would understand that she could not remain bound to him forever with another love in her heart. He would above all understand that at her age, twenty-three, what she needed was not diamond rivieres and bracelets, but necklaces of kisses and strings of caresses.

After the embrace, when she let Mario know about her plans to leave her husband, her lover sat up on an elbow, took a filter-tipped cigarette from the gold case she had given him at Christmas, lit it, and blew a cloud of smoke toward the ceiling. Then, he pronounced slowly and distinctly with his inimitable accent:

"But I'm already married in my country, darling."

And he added firmly, almost disdainfully:

"Yo tengo esposa en mi país. I have a wife in my country."

Coralie looked at him with horror, her mouth open in a silent cry. Then she dressed hurriedly, gathered up her stockings and her bag which lay on a sofa, and without even combing her hair, rushed toward her car. She drove like a mad woman until she got home, passing without seeing the the maid and the house boy who came running to help. She bounded into the living room to find herself face to face with Gratien who, feeling tired from hypoglycemia, rather common with diabetics, had come back earlier than usual on this particular Saturday.

Upon seeing her arrive with her dress badly fastened, her hair a mess, her stockings slung around her neck, her haggard look, her cheeks flushed from shame and anger, Gratien waited to calm her down, but she pushed him aside roughly and ran toward the stairs which she climbed four at a time, disposing of her shoes on the landing. He heard the bed she threw herself on creak beneath her agitated movements followed by the cry she suddenly released, the cry of an animal wounded in the entrails and which ended in sobs. Then he went upstairs, the pitiful, little gentleman with his grotesque appearance, yet still extraordinary with his quiet strength. With a nudge of his shoulder, he opened Coralie's door and approached her bed where she lay gasping, her eyes glued to the ceiling.

"Go away," shouts the woman. "Go away, you disgust me!"

Gratien spoke calmly:

"So, he has left you?"

Coralie turned a surprised glance toward her husband, a hunted animal's look where fear and amazement were visible. She hesitated for an instant. Then she mumbled:

"You ... you knew?"

"I have always known everything about you, my darling. I have suffered through you, for you, and with you."

"Gratien ...."

"I would have liked others to be able to give you this happiness that I myself was incapable of giving you, in spite of my tenderness, my love, my need to protect you. I have failed, and you are unhappy."

The good man took one of Coralie's hands and held it for a long time in his own. Little by little, Coralie calmed down. Her breathing became more regular. She continued to cry, but her tears were no longer as copious. Now they slipped out from the corners of her closed eyelids, ran slowly, slowly alongside her nose, only to disappear in the laces of her pillow case.

When he thought she had finally fallen asleep, Gratien bent over and placed a fervent kiss on her beautiful, smooth forehead and got up to leave. But Coralie was not sleeping. She clasped her husband's neck and drew him toward her. Elated with a happiness for which he had waited much too long, Gratien found her lips, and she returned his kiss. He hugged the beautiful body she offered him, and at last, for the first time, they rejoined and were husband and wife.

THE FIFTH STATION

DECEMBER 31: BIZOTON

NOON

Coralie descends laboriously along the road to the capital. Her tall body wavers in space every two seconds. The passers-by no longer make fun of her in this zone where her strange, disjointed silhouette and her broken jaw are the object of people's compassion. Only those who pass by in taxis on their way to Carrefour or in busses headed south continue to be surprised by this unusual, unsteady silhouette. The poor woman seems to be increasingly content with her state since, viewed from one side, her face is euphoric. Her strange, forced smile fascinates strangers who make bets on her fall. "Will she or won't she fall?" Where are her irregular steps taking her, this sad woman with the heron-like legs? It is the time of day when her shadow is fully gathered under her feet. An exacting noon-day sun reigns fire on her exposed skull where one can see her pale rose colored scalp. She is being literally cooked by the sun and arrives at Bizoton panting, winded, thirsty, drained. She plans to go and ask help from Marguerite, the old Rita from the Acapulco Bar and whose life has had a happy ending using the criteria by which Haitian society judges these things.

The vivacious whore from the brothel who loved to laugh voluptuously has become a chubby, heavy-jowled, big-breasted matron. She married a decent taxi driver who gave her three daughters and a cement and paint business from which she gets along so well that it seems she had never done anything else. Memories of the Acapulco Bar disappeared, the time of laughter and song, battles with rivals, the sensuous or lively tunes ground out by the jukebox, all forgotten. Madame Marguerite buried Rita. Rita dead and with her everything that might recall the era of good meals paid for by others and of ecstasy. Her taxi-driver husband cheats on her now with much younger, more slender girls, girls with firm buns and pointed breasts whom he takes to la Mer Frappée to swim and have a good feed at the "Trois Crabes." Sometimes he takes as many as three at a time for a Saturday evening or a Sunday noon wild party. When Marguerite sees him arrive disheveled and still a little drunk, she hurries to cut some lemons with which she rubs him vigorously behind the ears.

Sometimes he vomits on her. She couldn't care less. She would go through a thousand tougher experiences rather than return to the house of prostitution. *Ou fou, li mèt fè sal vle, Magrit pap kite'l.* Are you crazy? He can do whatever he wants. Magritte will not leave him. To lead once again the life of a *bouzen kafe*, a prostitute in a brothel, never. *Ki mele Magrit.* Magritte doesn't care about all that. She has money, owns her business, and not only satisfies her hunger but overeats. She does not know how much the rent, water, and electricity cost. And then she has three daughters who go to a Catholic girls school run by nuns. *Nanpwen anyen ki cho ki pa frèt.* There's nothing hot that doesn't cool off. When the man gets tired, then he'll stop. In the meantime, Magrit *fèk tanmen*, she stands steadfast. Her only small revenge is that on Saturdays Monsieur can never find any clean clothes. She makes sure that he never has clean underwear for his escapades. The laundry is never ready before Sunday morning. *La val nan pintad li avek rad sal yo, tou swe, tou bouke, tou santi su.* He can go to his escapades with dirty clothes, all sweaty, all wrinkled, and smelly. He deserves it. Magritte has forgotten that in her prime, she, too, was a prostitute. She wants to forget everything from her past and not have anything to do with her former co-workers. All of this explains how she welcomes Cora *Je Dajan*, Cora, the woman with pale silver eyes, Cora *la Manca*, Cora, the half-handed woman, who staggers towards her.

"Sa vye fanm blanch, po lanvè sa a bezwen? What does this old white-looking woman with her skin turned inside out want?"

Magritte feels nauseous when she sees Coralie. Give her quickly what she asks for so that she goes away quickly, quickly, quickly. And so that her husband— it's New Year's Eve, right— who is going to come home earlier than usual to get ready for two days of carousing, does not meet this outcast, this slut, who, in spite of her poverty, seems to have stayed somewhat aristocratic. Let's finish this business quickly. It is Magritte who summons Coralie who limps awkwardly in front of her store.

"Cora, what brings you here at this time? You're out in the middle of the day without a hat to protect you from the blazing sun. *Ki van ki mennen ou? Se van joudlan?* What wind blew you in? Is it the New Year's?"

"*Non se move van, mèt kay la pral mete m deyò demen si lwaye kay la pa peye.* No, it's not a good wind. The house owner will kick me out tomorrow. I've come to see if you can lend me some money?"

"Ah, Cora, *ou vin move lè, lavant pa bon senmenn sila a.* You came at a bad time. Sales are down this week. By the beginning of December, people had done their shopping for paint to spruce up the front of their houses, to do a little bit of cleaning. As for cement, it doesn't sell in December. *Semenn fèt, noun sou banbòch, yo pa sou bati kay.* During the holiday season, people are having fun, not building houses."

"Magritte, anything you'll give me will be all right. If it's not for the rent, it's for food. Or for transportation. *Lakay fè nwa nèt.* Things are not good at all."

Magritte, who wants to get rid of Cora as fast as possible before her husband arrives, feels uncomfortable; she is on pins and needles. She wants this embarrassing witness to her past life to leave as soon as she can.

"Jesus, Mary, Joseph, *mwen tande klakson Jacob.* I hear Jacob honking his horn. Please, Cora, get going. Here are ten gourdes. *Ale chè, ale pou ou pa kontre avek mouche a. Ale, Manman, ale.* Go on, my dear, so that you won't meet this man. Go, dear, go."

And she stuffs two five *gourde* bills into Coralie's shabby purse and pushes her on the shoulder so abruptly that she apologizes when Coralie just about falls down.

"Oh, excuse me, *se twòp kouraj wi mwen genyen,* maybe I'm a little too strong. Go, go, so I can get a little peace and quiet."

And ashamed just the same for her harshness and brutality, she adds with the trace of a smile that makes her two little, mouse-like eyes disappear into her fat face.

"*Ou a tounen apre lafèt, ma kite yon ti kichòy pou ou. Bòn ane!* You can come back after the holidays. I'll have something ready for you then. And Happy New Year!"

Coralie finally goes away with bent shoulders and a heavy heart. Rita is dead. Only Magritte remains.

SIX

Coralie finally knew the happiness of being totally loved by a non-egotistical being who was tender and gentle. Nivel had not lived twenty years as a widower like a secular monk, and he compensated for his lack of physical attractiveness by a knowledge of the female body that left Coralie fully happy and satisfied. That is to say that she had lost three years of her life in a rush, fluttering about like a butterfly drinking, smoking, dancing, and laughing with people who were not equal to her old, good-natured husband either for their goodness or generosity, or even for their knowledge of the art of loving.

Gratien Nivel, entirely happy as well, had regained better health. They spent their evenings listening to music, sharing readings, conversing delightfully about art and literature. Eminently cultured, the businessman was a brilliant conversationalist who had been terribly bored by the social events to which Coralie took pleasure in dragging him. Now he and his wife understood one another and, in a nutshell, loved one another with a deep, mutual tenderness, and each evening, they went upstairs to the conjugal bedroom where they had finally been reunited. Each time they made love, Coralie slept with the untroubled sleep of a contented woman, and in the morning, when Gratien had to get up before she did to go to his office, it is she who raised herself up on her elbow to receive the good-bye kiss that would keep her feeling calm and sheltered for the whole day.

Then she went back to bed, happy all over again. Even Aline's presence no longer managed to exasperate her. The frightful migraines had disappeared. Coralie was so thoroughly immersed in her conjugal happiness that she became friends again with everybody.

One year after their true wedding night, Coralie found herself pregnant. This became yet another occasion for her to discover another Gratien. The husband scarcely let his young wife's feet touch the floor. Radiant in her effortless pregnancy, Coralie wanted to continue to lead an active life, clattering down the stairs, lifting vases and piles of books, climbing a ladder to attach a curtain in the baby-to-be's room. She even drove the heavily-built station-wagon when necessary. Gratien would put a stop to these activities with a precautionary and protective gesture.

"Be careful, darling. This box is too heavy for you. Call Marcel to unload the car."

"Get down quickly from the ladder, Coralie. You're going to fall."

"Climb the ladder slowly, like that ... rung by rung, like that. Be careful."

On clear nights, they went together to take the walk called for by the doctor, and Gratien was moved to tears to see a Coralie, increasingly more awkward and more beautiful in her glowing motherhood, zigzagging in front of him on Babiole's slopes.

One morning in April, after a few hours without any complications, Coralie gave birth to a big, nine-pound boy named Gratien-Félix. Gratien for the father and Félix to please Félicien by using this derivation of his first name. But the little baby very quickly became Féfé for everyone and was adored by his father, who was extremely proud of this long-awaited fatherhood.

Coralie received an exceptionally beautiful diamond bracelet from her husband with a simple card: "Thanks, my love."

The case was nestled in an armful of fifty red roses.

"Why fifty roses, Gratien?" questioned the young mother.

"Because, my darling, I hope to live to be one hundred and to celebrate our golden wedding anniversary with you. After all, we only need forty-four more years."

"Oh, Gratien," responded Coralie laughingly, "You certainly think of everything."

The honor of being Féfé's godmother fell to Rose Darcey. Coralie would have preferred to have Lise Alphonsin, but she was pursuing her medical studies in pediatrics in France. So Rose was the god-mother alongside the contented grandfather, Félicien, who was exceptionally proud of this sponsorship.

The baptismal reception was imposing and lasted from noon until seven in the evening. Féfé, according to everyone, had not cried when they poured the holy water from the baptismal fonts on him just as he had not cried when he had tasted salt for the first time. Everyone agreed that this was a truly good sign. They placed the cradle on the verandah in a cool spot protected from the overly curious. Just the same, their so-called friends took great pleasure in admiring the baby whole heartedly:

"My dear, at Gratien's age, ou kwè pitit saa se pal? Do you think this is his baby?"

"Especially the way Coralie flirted around during that time."

"There are some men who are more stupid than others."

"Coralie was very lucky. Watch out. She's coming to the table right now."

And to embrace Coralie:

"My dear, congratulations. He's truly a superb baby."

"And the spitting image of his father. Sé tèt coupé! He is his father's living image!"

"Thank you, thank you. Have you had something to eat? There's the buffet."

"Let us catch our breath. There are so many good things. You have spoiled us."

"It's my pleasure! And thank you for your gifts for Gratien-Félix. Martine, your drinking cup is a marvel, and Jeanne's rattle, a goldsmith's gem."

And the day passed quietly like the springtime. Once the baby had been washed, fed, and put to bed, the family found itself alone once again in the small music room where the Pleyel piano Gratien had given Coralie for their last anniversary occupied a place of honor.

Then appearing hesitant, Aline interrupted with a honey-toned voice:

"Coralie dear, I have ... or rather, we have, your papa and I, a huge favor to ask of you."

"Always say what's on your mind, Mama. If it's possible, it's already granted."

"I didn't expect anything less from your heart of gold, my dear daughter. Here it is: your father's business is not what it used to be."

"And I'm getting old," adds Félicien.

"Not any older than I, dear father-in-law and friend," says Gratien with a pleasant, assured laugh.

"Yes," continued Aline sweetly, turning her weasel-like face toward Coralie. "Yes, here's how things are. We thought that since you have everything, thanks to Gratien ...."

" ... and because Féfé will be his father's only heir," continued Félicien

"I've thought, or rather, we have thought about asking you to give up your share of your father's inheritance in favor of Marceau."

"You know that your little brother adores you, but that he's timid, withdrawn, and doesn't dare show his feelings. In the past you were so distant with him. To make a long story short, if you wanted to, at the time of your husband's death (Oh! Forgive me, Gratien, but we

must be realistic), you will in all likelihood inherit his entire fortune, and your son after you. It stands to reason that you won't need the little bit of money that Félicien might eventually leave you while Marceau, he ...."

Surprised, Coralie looked at Aline, then at Félicien, and finally at Gratien who was smiling and nodding his head. Coralie looks at her husband quizzically.

"You knew about this matter?"

"Aline mentioned it to me just after the birth of our son."

"And you didn't say anything to me about it?"

"I honestly didn't think about it with the birth, the baptism, and everything else, but what difference does it make? I agree in principle, but the final decision rests with you, and you know that I approve of everything you do."

"Just like me with Aline," says Félicien complacently.

"So, if you agree, Gratien, I'll sign the document. Where and when will this take place?"

"Here, now." And Aline took a notarized document out of her handbag.

"I know ... In short, we know your kind-heartedness so very well my child that I ... that we have had the will prepared by our lawyer, and the notary, Mr. Hamel, was quite willing to hand it over to us so that you could sign it in your home.

"But the witnesses ...."

"They'll sign tomorrow. Félicien will get the signatures of his four employees in the store and our stratagem will have worked."

*Aline tried to make up for the word "stratagem" which had acci-
dently slipped out of her mouth, laughing in a self-conscious way and
simpering:*

*"Naturally, I'm saying that jokingly, because there is no stratagem
involved here as you know very well."*

*Coralie looked at her husband anxiously for the last time, but Aline
was already pushing a small table toward her on which the re-
nouncement of her father's heritage, anchored by a heavy, onyx
ashtray, lay spread out.*

*"Well now, here's a pen ... rats, it doesn't have any ink. Nivel, lend
us your pen."*

*Gratien himself put his gold-plated pen in the trembling fingers of
Coralie who signed while steadying her right hand with her left. Up
until this time she had never imagined that someday her father or
Gratien would die leaving her rich or poor according to circumstances. Having signed, Coralie looked at Gratien once again. A
vague anxiety wrung her heart. Nivel reassured her with a glance:*

*"It's all right, my darling, it's better like that. Aline is right. Félix and
you will never be deprived of anything either while I'm living or after
my death. Let's go, come on, it's time for you to rest. The day has
been trying for a young mother. Come along, my love. Good-night,
Aline. Good-night, Félicien. Pleasant dreams."*

*Coralie kissed Aline's cheek and Félicien's forehead and took
Gratien's arm to return to their quarters. What would have been her
concern had she been able to see the disturbing, triumphal glimmer
that lit up Aline Santeuil's dark pupils.*

■ ■ ■ ■ ■

One year to the day after Félix's baptism, Gratien Nivel died suddenly at work from a heart attack. When the employees rushed into their bosses' office, his heart had stopped beating, and they had to inform Coralie and her parents.

The young woman's despair was deep. She had already been buffeted by life, and now her protector, friend, and husband had been taken from her just as they were beginning a new life with their child. He never had the chance to get to know his child. Who in her life could replace her kind, generous, understanding husband who, at the same time, had been an admirable companion, a substitute father?

Aline was simply calculating and hypocritical; Félicien, a limp rag dominated by his wife; Marceau, an unemotional, ambitious young cheat. No, Coralie did not have a family. Her old friend, Rose Darcey Leblanc, was not particularly supportive and of little help. Lise Alphonsin, who could have stood by her in her misfortune, was far away in France.

… France, that's it. Leave, travel. She had to leave, go far away, see some other countries, break away from the gang of shallow, greedy pleasure seekers who had just about destroyed her household and who wouldn't miss the chance to band together to devour Nivel's inheritance.

As legal beneficiary, she left Nivel's business to his business manager, entrusted his papers to a lawyer, instructed him to deposit a generous, monthly sum with Aline for her son's support, provided him with the necessary power of attorney to allow him to send her a comfortable allowance, and embarked two months later on the Royal Mail which sailed for England and France.

And Félix, a sixteen-month old baby? He is a nuisance for a young woman who wants to see the world. Thinking that she would come back in several months, Coralie imprudently entrusted Félix to Aline Santeuil, who took up her role of impromptu grandmother with delight and pride.

THE SIXTH STATION

DECEMBER 31: MARTISSANT

1:00 P.M.

The woman passing by on the Feast of St. Sylvester took a lengthy rest in the shade of some trees facing the Royal Quisqueya Hotel. It is pleasant and cool there, and Cora spent a long time watching the sea and the little boats, whose sails were like wings dancing on the turquoise waves. Why did her life not unfold calmly and steadily like this water lapping sea-green swirls so close to her feet? It would be so good to sleep in the arms of this sea which seems at the moment to be utterly gentle and calm. One moment, Cora is tempted to slide into the water and let herself go gently without even feeling the drowning. Another moment, she approaches the water to lose herself, already feeling its velvety embrace around her scraggy body.

She leans over the lapping slime and makes out something floating and gently rocking, and she sees, to her horror, a child's corpse, a several-month old fetus enveloped in a hideous mucus. Her heart freezes; she becomes frightened and steps back. And suddenly, her stomach curls up and she vomits. Seated at the foot of a tree where she props up her head, she takes out her handkerchief and wipes her mouth. The taste of the vomit still lingers between her tongue and her palate. She swallows several times to get rid of the bitter taste.

Then she thinks that, somewhere, in one of these coastal hovels, a girl pulled this cumbersome load from her womb. Perhaps some-where some woman cried for help, and she bled to death for lack of timely aid. Or perhaps even a drunk beat his pregnant mistress so much that the child broke loose from the womb and, scared, the wretched man threw the child into the sea.

Coralie thinks about all that, and she tells herself that the same thing could have happened to her, that she too could have aborted a child, or been beaten by her lover until she lost the baby, or even resorted to an illegal abortion with a rusty hanger playing havoc with her womb. She thinks that if she had not had Lise Alphonsin's help in time that she would have tried to get rid of the unwanted child, this Robert whom she loves at a distance, this boy conceived at a period in her life when, happy to be alive, she still believed in mankind and good fortune.

And she thinks about this other child swimming under the water, the child who might have known a home somewhere. She thinks about the poor mother, dead perhaps, or permanently sterilized for her folly, forced by hunger and the cruel world to stifle her maternal dreams.

She, the poor outcast, Cora la Manca, the beggar woman, cries for a long time about the fate of an unknown woman who resembles her like a sister; she cries about the child who will never have known the love and the tenderness of a mother's heart. Cora, the reprobate, cries for a long time.

Little unborn child, Coralie Santeuil was your sad mother for an hour.

Coralie now reaches Manigat Street in Martissant. She is coming to see Madame Arsène, her former landlady from happier days, days over and done with, when she was a plucky, efficient, hard-working, honest woman. Coralie wants to ask her for a loan, but what pawn can she give to the worthy shopkeeper? *Bay se bay, men prete se remet.* A gift is a gift, but when you borrow something, you have to return it.

Madame Arsène listens to the long litany of Coralie's misfortunes.

"Mais hélas, chè pitit an mwen, mwen pa sa ede ou non. Ou sonje Sylvanne ti nyes mwen an sa ki te kon tire bèf la pou ou, li mouri wi, anvanyè. But alas, my dear, I really can't help you. Do you remember my little niece, Sylvanne, who used to milk the cow for you? She died the day before yesterday. *Li fè yon pèdisyon, emoraji pote l ale. Yon si jèn ti fi, si travayant, li kite gason vire tèt li: gwosès, avòtment, lanmò!* She had a miscarriage, and she died of a hemorrhage. A very young girl, hard working, she let some guy fool around with her and bingo, she got pregnant, had a miscarriage, and then comes Death!"

Sylvanne, the mischievous child who laughed until she cried when the cow splashed her with streams of frothy milk. Coralie blends her sighs with the abundant tears shed by Madame Arsène about the fate of the foolish Sylvanne. Upon leaving, the grocer gives Cora three *dous lèt*, some milk candy, and slips her five five-*gourde* bills, five dollars. She says it is all of her earnings since this morning.

So Cora sets out again, limping, while thinking about the fetus that sleeps over there in the lapping of the sea-green water with its metallic, greenish glints.

SEVEN

France, Le Havre, September, 1938. On the ship the night before arriving, Coralie had celebrated her twenty-seventh birthday with champagne and music on the last evening on board. Her red-haired beauty had never been more resplendent. She relished the pleasure of being surrounded, adulated, and courted; she definitely made up her mind to take full advantage of all of the pleasures that Parisian life might offer a beautiful, free, financially independent young woman.

She was therefore impressed to find the French capital in a festive mood. The Munich Accords had just been signed with Hitler, and the two capitulators, Daladier and Chamberlain, who expected to be hissed for their weak behavior before the German Führer, were totally surprised to find themselves welcomed with the joyful shouts of a crowd who chanted their names to the rhythm of the cries for "Long Live Peace." In the enthusiastic streets they traveled through, standing up in open cars, British and French flags flapped in the autumn wind, and street dances continued all night long.

Coralie was fascinated by so many expressions of public joy. She had never seen anything like this in Haiti where she had lived a cloistered life, first in boarding school, then in Aline Santeuil's residence, and finally, spoiled and protected by Gratien Nivel whose death, scarcely one year after the birth of their son, had caused her deep sorrow.

But she was in good health, she was rich, and her youthfulness spoke to her in a loud, clear voice. It said to her:

"Take advantage of this moment. Take advantage of your good years. Life is short, and you must hurry to enjoy it."

She initially intended to have only a short, six-month stay in Europe before returning home and reclaiming her son from Aline. But how does one tear oneself away from Paris and its pleasures, especially if one has also decided to visit Rome and Naples, Madrid and Toledo, London and Stratford, Berlin and Munich, Vienna and Salzburg, without mentioning other important places in the world of art and culture?

And then, all the men encountered since the crossing, everywhere in the world of the easy, gay life that reigned in Europe in wealthy circles, seemed to her to be Adonis, Eros, and Apollo in great numbers, destined from the outstart to console pretty widows who wore black and gray so becomingly.

In Paris itself, Coralie Nivel quickly established her habits. Staying in a luxurious suite at the Grand Hôtel, people saw her at the theater where she applauded Giraudoux, Salacrou, and Guitry. After that, with a group of new friends, those parasites always attracted by wealth, she went to dinner at Maxim's or at the Tour d'Argent. In the afternoon, she was already accepted at Fouquet's and Claridge's, where she had tea while talking about Pagnol's latest play, Jacques Feydeau's latest film, or the really terrific loose-fitting suits just launched by Mademoiselle Gabrielle Chanel.

"Just think, darling, that she refused to marry the Duke of Westminster."

"You think it was Westminster, darling? To be more precise, wasn't it Bedford?"

"Bedford or Westminister, it's all the same thing to us French. In any case, she refused to become a duchess saying that there were duchesses everywhere in England, but that there was only one Coco Chanel in the world."

"And she is perfectly right."

And they laughed and gossiped in the smoke from long, golden, mother-of-pearl cigarette lighters, inset with imitation precious stones, marketed by Paul Poiret, already relegated to obscurity by Chanel, Patou, Fath, and Molyneux.

Coralie lived this frivolous, perfumed life for one long, laughter and song-filled year. The music hall was in full swing, and Mistinguett gave way to Josephine Baker, who in order to give an example of harmony, adopted twelve children of different races whom she raised in her castle close to Paris with her husband, Jo Bouillon, the orchestra leader. At Paris' casino, his straw hat askew, wearing tails and bow tie, Maurice Chevalier puckered his waggish, lower lip singing "Ma Pomme" while an enthusiastic audience picked it up and sang along. The war? Come on. The Führer had said it well. Once the Sudètes in Czechoslovakia were returned to the large Germanic family, he no longer had any territorial claims in Europe. Mussolini, the Italian Duce, another signer of the Munich Accord, guaranteed it. And western Europe, carefree and happy, continued to sail toward its destiny. From time to time, one certainly heard people talking about the USSR, but was not Russia, inspected and chastised, a natural ally of France against Germany? To be sure, there was the question of purges, massacres, and the iron grip of a certain Stalin, but who worried about that? Moscow is truly far away and springtime is so beautiful in Paris.

And in the summertime, vacation time, the famous paid holidays made available since 1936 by the Front Populaire, "Popu-Roi" as Henri Béraud used to say, hadn't yet inundated the uncongested highways with vacationing hoards. St. Tropez was still just a little fishing village where Colette had recently bought herself a summer villa. La Croisette was still populated with English noblemen and thin gentlewomen with big feet and long teeth who required chaperons, and with a string of young lords and ladies in sport shorts with their tennis rackets. There, people were from the same social class, and they spoke a lot about young Madame Nivel, the youthful, beautiful widow from Haiti.

"Haiti? Where is it, my dear? In Oceania?"

"Definitely not, my dear. You're mixing it up with Tahiti."

"Haiti is in the Antilles, in America."

"They are all black countries, my dear."

"So how do you explain the fact that she's so white?"

"And so rich?"

Unaware of the curiosity that her fortune, beauty, and fair skin aroused, Coralie fully enjoyed the carefree life she was leading, traveling in her rented De Dion Bouton with a chauffeur in uniform and a maid, and finally bored with the French Riviera, she visited Italy. She applauded Toscanini at La Scala in Milan, and Benjamin Gigli, who made people forget the great Caruso, at San Carlo in Naples. From the beautiful, old city of Naples, she took an excursion to Capri's blue caves, Pompeii's touching ruins, and then Rome's Trevi Fountain where visitors throw good-luck coins, making Roman strollers happy.

Returning to France along the Riviera, she left for Spain to visit Madrid's Prado Museum and its famous collection of works by Goya and Velasquez; Toledo and El Greco's house; Seville and the royal tombs of Isabella and Ferdinand; and then the coast of the Spanish Riviera—Cadix, Malaga, Murcie, Valencia, Alicante, and finally Barcelona, where she was present for the fireworks on the Montjuich hill on the Feast of St. John. She didn't come back to France until September, l939. The war, the hideous war, had broken out on September 1 with the invasion of Poland by Hitler, still more greedy for indispensable space. Where would this famous "Lebensraum" stop? In the meantime, Europe went up in flames.

Elated by her effortless life and persuaded that France and England were strongly prepared for a war against Nazi Germany, Coralie did not hurry to return to Haiti. Crossings became less frequent, and then, on the whole, the war was going on over there, in the East. On the Western front, nothing or next to nothing was happening, and the war bogged down, purring like a big, well-fed cat in the corner of the fireplace.

The "phony" war lasted nine months from September, l939, to May, l940. The Soviet-German non-aggression pact had surprised the Western world and had allowed Hitler to swallow up Poland, divided with Stalin, in a single, big, gluttonous mouthful. Free in the East, Hitler turned subsequently against France and England who, in their complacent tranquillity, had done nothing for nine months to strengthen their obsolete, ill-assorted armaments.

And suddenly, the onslaught ensued. The Panzer divisions moved into Belgium and the North of France with an indomitable thrust.

Handsome officers, like some young gods from Valhalla, descended from heaven fully outfitted with boots and helmets, leading an infantry assault on out-moded France, their divisions sweeping aside everything on the road to victory. Devoured, its king disconcerted by the weakness of its so-called allies, Belgium was forced to surrender. On May 10 it was France's turn to be let down. In spite of the desperate efforts of Weygand, named to replace a discredited and dismissed Gamelin, in spite of the individual heroism of certain officers like Colonel Charles de Gaulle, France was brought to its knees and forced to ask for an armistice. Marshall Pétain took power governing a part of France, a free zone that would prove to be a mixed blessing.

Like the mongrel that bites slyly from behind, Italy appropriated a good portion of the Midi, in particular Nice, Nizza, the city so sorely missed and coveted. France, cut into pieces and gasping for breath, was on the verge of collapse. The voice of a simple general with a provisional title who spoke from London with a jerky, muffled voice was only heard by a very small number of French patriots from among the extremely limited number who believed in a final victory in spite of the actual disaster.

This situation was catastrophic for Coralie Santeuil. Given her state of well being, her giddy joie de vivre, and the flood of praise surrounding her, she had voluntarily ignored the advance warning signs of the French collapse, and now she was trapped, stuck, unable to go back to Haiti. One by one, communications between France and the rest of the world were interrupted more often leaving this beautiful country isolated and powerless under the Nazi boot. The heroic English resistance to the Blitzkrieg had blocked Hitler's advance, but for how long? The conflict expanded. After Poland, Memel and the Baltic States fell. Denmark, Norway, Holland, Luxembourg, and then Greece, Cyprus, and eventually North Africa. In their euphoria over the Wehrmacht's repeated victories, the Nazis did not take note of Hitler's monumental blunder. Like Napoleon 130 years earlier, he made the mistake of striking deep into the Russian steppes without accounting for those three invincible Russian generals: Space, Time, and Winter.

Apparently nothing could stop Hitler, and France succumbed to the increasingly more difficult yoke of the Nazi occupation. For collabo-

rators, life was still filled with pleasures, and they could find every-thing on the black market provided they were willing to pay the price. Coralie resigned herself to not being able to return to her distant island, but not a single bank draft could reach her. She was forced to look for a more modest apartment, return the rented car, and dismiss the expensive chambermaid in charge of her affairs. Coralie did not know how to cook a hard-boiled egg nor how to hold a feather duster. Even though she hired a housekeeper who came twice a week to do the heavy work, the upkeep of her modest apartment on the Rue Racine quickly proved much too costly for her debt-ridden finances. She looked for work, but what did Madame Nivel know how to do? For a time, thanks to her exotic beauty, glowing skin, red hair, slender silhouette, and immense, pale-blue eyes, she was hired as a model in the fashion houses where she had once been a customer. She went from Jacques Fath's to Molyneux's, from Maggy Rouff's to Balenciaga's, but one by one the showrooms closed for lack of clients, especially those wealthy American women who were compelled subsequently to find clothing in New York and Boston. Because of her intermittent work schedule, Coralie saw the last resources in her bank account disappear. One day, she was compelled to go to a jeweler in Rue de la Paix to sell the diamond riviere that Gratien had given her at Félix's baptism. She managed for about two months with the money, but the scarcity of food and the increased black market prices didn't enable her to cover her total expenses. She had to give up her apartment and be satisfied with an attic room in the upper reaches of the Rue Lepic. Life was tolerable and less expensive than in the Latin Quarter, but no one knew for how long. Not knowing either how to sew or cook, she ate in a bar in Montmartre and became an artist's model. On the Place du Tertre, artists, as poor as they were talented, gave her several francs for painting her face and her hands, but others were bold enough to invite her to their studios where they painted her naked, stretched out on an Oriental carpet or posing as a woman taking a bath. The studios were badly heated and the bearded painters seductive. Coralie experienced momentary ecstasy in the arms of strapping art students who smelled like red wine and bad tobacco, but who made love like gods. Afterwards, they went to have a cup of unsweetened chicory on the terrace of a cafe whose windows were shaded with strips of blue paper. There they waited until curfew before going back to a chilly, little bedroom. The nights when Coralie didn't return to the Rue Lepic, she slept with one or another of these artist-lovers *trying to keep each other warm by lying close together. In the fireplaces they burned newspaper pellets that produced little heat and gave off irritating smoke that brought tears to their eyes.*

Coralie liked this life without security, without real attachments, almost without resources. Living this way, she developed a taste for the Bohemian life, learning to drink bad, impure wine straight from the bottle. She smoked strong tobacco, Gitanes and Gauloises, whose smoke could not be compared to the mild aroma of the Pall Malls and Lucky Strikes that she had smoked rather infrequently in Port-au-Prince. Alcohol and tobacco entered her life never to leave it.

All the same, life became more and more difficult for Coralie who had been used to comforts her artist friends were only vaguely familiar with. Sometimes she felt like going to a fashionable place, dressing elegantly, and putting on her last furs for a dinner at Maxim's.

It was there one evening that she met Major Klaus von Dieter, an officer in the Wehrmacht stationed in Paris. This descendent of a noble French Huguenot family that had fled France at the time of the Revocation of the Edict of Nantes was a perfect gentleman with exquisite manners and a sophisticated education. He saw Coralie dining alone in a corner of the famous restaurant's large dining room. He was alone as well. He got up, approached the young woman, clicked his heels, and introduced himself:

"Major von Dieter."

Coralie gazed at the handsome officer who bowed his stately height before her. It was Wotan himself in the gray uniform accented with red.

"Coralie Nivel."

"May I offer you a glass of champagne."

Champagne! Even though she was seated at Maxim's, Coralie, during this period of poverty, could no longer afford champagne.

"Of course you may, Major. But please do sit down."

Major von Dieter took off his gray gloves, snapped his fingers, and an eager, excessively polite waiter rushed up.

"A bottle of Dom Perignon, 1908," he ordered with the authority of a connoisseur increased twofold by his status as a high-ranking German officer. The precious bottle was brought to them, wrapped in a white napkin in a silver bucket wreathed in condensation.

"If you give me permission, pretty lady, I'll drink to the most beautiful eyes in the world," he said after having filled two tall champagne flutes with the sparking, golden liquid.

She heard herself answer mischievously:

"To your loves, Major."

"From now on, that will depend on you, pretty lady."

He questioned Coralie skillfully, asked her for information about Haiti and her family, and inquired about where she had gotten her pale azure eyes and her flaming, copper-colored hair. They were talking when she suddenly became anxious:

"The curfew ...."

" ... doesn't exist for me, dear friend, and if you agree to keep me company, then I'll bring you back to your residence."

And they spent an unforgettable night together at the Ritz getting to know one another, each elated with the other's beauty. Their liaison was tumultuous, passionate, and soon known by all of the Parisian collaborators. They were seen together at the theater; at Ambassador Otto Abetz's receptions; at the Kommandantur; at von Choltitz's, the governor of greater Paris; and at cocktail parties at the Hôtel Lutetia, the headquarters for German officers stationed in Paris. They did not invite Major von Dieter without the beautiful Haitian and vice versa. Cora's high-society friends once again became interested in her with the unavowed goal of using her influence on the handsome German major to obtain relief from the extremely strict rules of the occupying forces.

Cora had completely forgotten her dubious dealings in Montmartre and her art student friends so lacking in brilliance. But if she saw the signature of one of her former lovers in a lower corner of a landscape at an art dealer's, she praised the work's pictorial qualities to von Dieter, and urged him to buy the canvas. This was her way of helping the poor artists who had kept her warm when she needed it, and a way of being forgiven and of forgiving herself for her relationship with a German, however civilized he might be.

On June 6, 1944, the Allies finally landed in Normandy. Germany had already lost its foothold in Russia and found itself facing a second front. Collaborators of every stripe became frightened and lost their insolent arrogance.

When coming back one evening to the furnished studio apartment the Major had rented for her on Rue de la Pompe in the fashionable sixteenth arrondissement, she found this inscription in capital letters stuck to her door:

"German's whore, we'll have you skinned."

Coralie became frightened. Major von Dieter loved Coralie sincerely and wanted to protect her from the fate awaiting women who had prostituted themselves to the Germans. Like most highly commissioned officers, he regarded Hitler as a dangerous madman, and he knew that Germany had lost the war. While continuing to do his duty as a soldier, he set in motion everything he could to shelter his pretty mistress from the reprisals of the Resistance, which each day was becoming more active and more efficient in the occupied zone. Now that the whole of France had been invaded and that there was no longer an unoccupied zone, he arranged to send Coralie towards the south, where their showy liaison was undoubtedly less well known. For greater security, Coralie took back her maiden name, Santeuil. The seductive Madame Nivel was too familiar in certain circles. During their last encounter, von Dieter asked her:

"Do you know anyone, somewhere, anywhere in the former non-occupied zone in the south?"

"No … or rather, yes, I suppose so. Before the war, I had a very good Haitian girl friend, Lise Alphonsin, studying medicine in Montpellier."

With discretion, von Dieter pulled some administrative strings and found out that "Yes, Dr. Alphonsin was still in Montpellier. She had married a young Jewish intern, who was deported and died at Drancy. She lived alone, had no children, and was actively engaged in caring for Belgian and French refugee children in a camp in the south."

In a short time, Coralie, once again named Santeuil, was sent south to Montpellier in a special convoy transporting important archives. Lise Alphonsin had received a confidential message asking her to welcome her friend and to lodge with her until further orders. Orders that never came. The liberation of the French territory occurred with its parade of heroism, retaliation, injustice, and vengeance, a mixture of the grandiose and the sordid. Trembling with fear, Coralie followed the story of the women associated with German soldiers who were shaved, tonsured, and dragged naked through the streets by a enraged populace. Fortunately for her, no one knew her in the medical circles in which Lise moved. The latter had definitely decided to go back to her country to work for the amelioration of health conditions for Haitian children. With nothing more keeping them in France, Lise, who was exceptionally resourceful, succeeded in obtaining two places on a cargo ship scheduled to leave Bordeaux for New York. From there, they were to sail on a small, French cargo ship called the "Canche" which plied between New York and Port-au-Prince carrying freight and a maximum of twelve passengers.

In this way Coralie Santeuil returned to her country in February, 1946. Her absence, planned for six months, had lasted eight years.

THE SEVENTH STATION

DECEMBER 31: JEAN JACQUES DESSALINES BOULEVARD

4:00 P.M.

Exhausted, Coralie sits for a long time on the edge of the metal fountain which interrupts Manigat Street and marks the spot where the villa of the general who gave his name to this road once stood.

The flight of steps in front of the former sumptuous residence of one of Haiti's most renowned potentates is now incorporated into a state school. It is almost two o'clock and the day moves along. The school is empty, the little girls are on vacation. Coralie ate the three candies given to her by Madame Arsène a long time ago, and now an intense thirst makes her tongue feel parched. A little girl about ten years old passes by carrying an enormous plastic bucket from which trickles a spurt of water at each step. At the rate she is going, Coralie thinks, she will have almost no water in this container when she arrives at her destination, and she will be beaten and sent back again to the fountain. No book has taught Cora about the fate of underprivileged children in our midst, the children working as domestics called *restavek*. She thinks about how much her childhood was sheltered in spite of Aline and the others. She always ate her fill, always had a place to shelter herself and to sleep. So Coralie calls the youngster who shifts her weight from side to side under the overly heavy load.

"E, tifi, *little girl*, come here."

"*Sa pou fèm granmoun?* What do you want me for, old woman?"

"*Vann mwen ti gout dlo.* Sell me some water."

"*Dlo sila a pa pou vann.* This water is not for sale."

"*Tanpri, mwen swaf anpil.* Please, I'm really thirsty."

At first distrustful, the timid child approaches:

"What are you going to drink it out of? Do you have a cup?"

And Coralie holds out the crippled hand she usually hides, because the afflicted fingers are curled as if fused together to form a permanent hollow so that when she extends her right hand, she always seems to be holding out a dried calabash, a *koui* to be more exact, the *koui* of the beggar that she is going to become, that she is already becoming. The youngster seems to be moved to pity, and Coralie helps her tip the pail and painfully collects two or three gulps of water in the hollow of her hand that she laps up eagerly.

"*Mèsi anpil pitit mwen, mèsi* ... Thanks a lot, my little one, thanks ... *Tann, map ba ou yon ti bagay.* Wait, I'm going to give you something."

And rummaging around in her old handbag, she holds out a dollar, a five gourde, very new, very red bill to the surprised little girl. The kid cannot believe her eyes. Five gourdes for her all by herself! Some New Year's gift, some honest-to-goodness New Year's gift! She is going to be able to buy herself some candy for New Year's Day, tons of barley candy, tons of balloons. Then she thinks that she will have to hide her treasure *"byen fon, fon, fon, fon* .... Very deep, deep, deep so that the lady I work for doesn't know where it is because she would take it away."

Coralie helps the youngster readjust her exceptionally heavy pail on the *trokèt*, a head piece, made from dirty rags rolled into a crown. The child leaves, joyfully, suddenly walking on air, happy about the good fortune for which, her joy being so great, she has forgotten to thank *la vieille dédé à la main pòk*, the old lady with the crippled hand.

"Maybe she's paralyzed", she says to herself, somewhat scared by the strange deformity.

With great difficulty, Coralie now crosses the puddles of that dirty water which never drains at the entrance to Bicentenaire Avenue. Her perforated shoes take in the lukewarm muddy water at each step. Once at the gas station, she asks for a little water to wash herself. She can't go on like this with dirty feet. This woman who has lost her social position has not lost her taste for cleanliness. Her heart sinks seeing the youngsters who, with a string and an empty paint bucket, draw filthy water right from the stinking, wide-open drain. They use it to wash the tires of the *camionnettes*, the station wagons parked at the gas station for the small change the drivers of those cabs called *"La Fontaine de Siloé*, Siloam's Fountain" or *"Mèsi l'Eternel*, Thanks, Eternal One" casually throw them while driving away. To her horror they also wash themselves with the same water, laughing in their shabby clothing and hitting each other playfully with big, wet rags.

"So much misery, so many children to save, Lord. What an immense task."

And she remembers the joy of the youngster who was so delighted with the dollar she has given her. At last, she may satisfy her hunger for a day. Hunger. Coralie feels desperately hungry at this time of the afternoon. At Portail Léogâne, she could buy herself a bowl of *manje kwit*, ready-made food, for little money, but up until now, in her material distress, she has not been able to get used to eating these *chen jambe*, the food exposed to passing dogs that abound on the sidewalks. Coralie is sick to her stomach from the dust, the flies, the mud. Instead, she is going to walk as far as St. Paul's Bakery on Grande Ru. There she will be able to buy herself something nourishing, good smelling, and piping hot from the oven wrapped in clean paper.

She still has six dollars. With that she will be able to eat several pâtés, a piece of cake, drink a nicely chilled cola, and still have enough for transportation to continue her long December quest.

She now skirts sidewalks congested with containers of merchandise. The female venders' displays are loaded with inexpensive toys; Florida water; very strongly, too strongly perfumed soaps; and very violently, too violently tinted face powders. Brightly colored scarves hanging at the shop doors barely allow clients to pass. She is jostled by a peddler carrying a huge cardboard box full of flashlights, shoelaces, sunglasses, key chains, cigarette lighters, and padlocks. Bumped roughly on the shoulder by the box, Coralie starts, and a lighter falls and suddenly breaks, spilling a volatile liquid. The peddler shouts:

"Look at how this old lady has made me lose my merchandise. Look at your face, white cockroach, sorceress. You're going to pay me. *Kale m kòb mwen oswa map wonpi ou ak baton.* Pay me or I'll beat you to death."

Coralie gets out of trouble with ten gourdes from her insignificant savings. Half of the day has slipped away, and she still has not succeeded in getting a loan or a gift enabling her to appease the frightening Cétoute Ti Bidon with even an advance, a deposit allowing her to keep her room. She must find the sum before nightfall, and once more Coralie sighs just as she had in the morning:

"Félix ... Robert ... Alas!"

Hunger makes her shrinking stomach growl. She goes into the St. Paul Bakery where she relishes several piping hot meat-filled pastries followed by a slice of extremely fresh cake. She drinks a well-chilled Darco cola. Refreshed, she feels stronger and ready to take to the road again, although she has only ten gourdes left in her possession.

She now walks out under the bakery's porch between two displays that only leave room for a pair of human feet. She lowers her head to see clearly where she is placing her unruly legs and to avoid over-turning or breaking anything, which would deplete her resources.

As she raises her head, she sees them.

A shouting crowd is there booing someone. Who are they attacking in this way? What pickpocket? What daring thief?

No, the shouting mob is pursuing her:

"*Men li, men sòsyè a, men lougawou a.* There she is, this witch!"

She is showered with insults and, as she anticipates, the blows follow. What do they have against her? Have they mistaken her for somebody else? But who could possibly look like the tall, gray-haired woman with a crooked face and a disjointed walk?

All of a sudden, the crowd pushes a crying, little girl in front of her. It is the youngster with the water pail from Manigat Street. The crying child, whose big tears run down her face, snuffles the mucus dripping from her nose toward her swollen lips, evidence that she had been the brunt of lots of slaps and smacks in the face. The child gasps:

"Here's the money you lent me. I'm paying it back."

Cora can barely utter:

"*Poukisa, sak pase?* Why? What happened?"

"*Gen moun wouj ki konn bay timoun lajan pou yo ka manje yo.* Some fair-skinned people give little kids money so they can eat them. *Men pran kòb ou.* Here, take your money."

With a sudden burst of pride, Coralie takes the bill and hurls back:

"*Mwen pa manje tout vyann.* I don't eat all kinds of meat!"

The cries, the shouts begin all over again while she tries to get out of the way, maneuvering between the street stalls.

"*Sòsyè!* Sorceress!"

"*Lougawou!* Witch!"

"*Satan jerenons* … She Devil …"

Garbage and peelings begin to shower on her. If the sidewalks provided stones, she would be killed. A grapefruit peel pulled out of the gutter hits her in the middle of the back and stains her shabby dress. Coralie flees in the pelting storm. She got back five gourdes but lost her last illusions.

EIGHT

Once back in her own country, Coralie stayed in a boarding house. Then she went to her parents' home principally to see her father and her son once again. Such a long absence must have displeased them all. Aline had not changed: skinny, wrinkled, harsh, sarcastic. Félicien was a septuagenarian whose health had deteriorated a great deal and who had abandoned all activity. Coralie found him in front of his radio, one foot in a slipper, the other, whose big, swollen toe indicated an attack of gout, resting on a small footstool. He looked at her with dull eyes, his thick, lower lip flabby, his nose inordinately elongated. Without emotion or surprise, he blurted out at Coralie:

"Well, it's you. You haven't gained any weight."

And this was the only welcome she received from this father she continued to cherish in spite of his listlessness. As for Aline, she received her stepdaughter in the living room like a visitor just passing through. She asked her why she had stayed out of the country for such a long time. Surprised and shocked, Coralie answered:

"But there was the war, a terrible war in Europe."

"Don't imagine that we are completely ignorant on this side of the Atlantic. We knew about it, but eight years! You must have been enjoying yourself in France so that you didn't make any effort to come back?"

And Aline cited the names of three or four families the war had also taken by surprise in Europe and who, thank God (and Aline lifted her eyes heavenward), had managed to come back home.

"It's true that these people were concerned about their elderly parents and didn't want to abandon their child. As for you, my poor daughter ...."

And Aline sighed in a way that indicated she knew what she was saying.

"But Aline ...."

Saying "Mama Line" was no longer possible for Coralie.

" ... but Aline, communications were cut off, and the only thing left to do was to wait."

"To wait, but with what means? It's true that a pretty, young woman ... In the end, you came out of it without too much damage based on what I can see. Ou anfòm net, you're really in good shape; even though people were saying that food was scarce in Europe! Right?"

And Aline clicked her tongue in disbelief. In her jealous frame of mind, it is as if Aline had an inkling that such a beautiful girl had not had any trouble finding zealous admirers to feed her, dress her, and shelter her in hard times in exchange for favors.

Coralie felt herself blush right down to her scalp. Is it possible that some gossips had alerted Aline to her life with the painters in Montmartre and her notorious liaison with the German officer? She coughed to restore her voice and change the subject:

"May I see Félix? Where is he?"

"It's a school day, my dear. Ou byen wè ou se touris. One can clearly see that you're a tourist. The child is in class at St. Martial's. Believe it or not, he is nine years old."

"When can I see him?"

"He comes home at five o'clock after sports. It would be better if you came back tomorrow, Saturday, because I need to give him some advance notice. He doesn't know you, not even from photos. It's going to be a shock for the little fellow when he sees a totally unknown mother appear from out of nowhere. What a shame. Not even one photo in eight years!"

And once again, Aline sighed at length. Exasperated, Coralie resumed the conversation with veiled anger:

"I've already told you that there was a war going on and no way of communicating."

"Oh yes, the war. Just the same, you spent more than a year before the conflict parading around Europe living lavishly. More than a year when you could have at least sent a decent photo to your child if you had wanted him to remember you."

Aline—always logical, always relentless. Coralie would definitely never have the last word with her stepmother. She preferred to change the subject and inquired:

"And Marceau?"

"He's fine. He just became engaged to a very proper young lady."

"And his business dealings?"

"Good without being excellent. The Santeuil family made some good deals during the war because we had stock. But Marceau has been making some changes since last year. Everything needs to be rebuilt in the world, and everything needs to be rebuilt in Haiti. He is also transforming your father's business more and more and moving into construction materials. As soon as he can, he'll eliminate the wines, fine soaps, and other luxury items. He says that the future is elsewhere."

"In short, is he happy?"

"Yes, on the whole."

Tackling now the subject of her assets left behind in Haiti at the time of her departure for Europe in 1938, Coralie inquired:

"And my house at Pacot?"

"Rented to a foreign diplomat, a Colombian to be precise. It's with that money that I cover Félix's expenses, because your lawyer ...."

"What about my lawyer?"

"As far as I'm concerned, your Mr. Hamel is a common crook. He's made some shady deals with your papers, and I suspect that there isn't much left of Gratien's estate."

Aline clenched her teeth and narrowed her lips to a slit. She hissed between her teeth:

"That's what happens when you don't listen to your parents. When leaving, you preferred trusting strangers. You let outsiders take care of your business. So right now, sa ou pran se pa ou, whatever happens to you, you deserve."

"What? Mr. Hamel?" stammered Coralie.

"D'ailleurs, besides, if you don't believe it, that's your business. A young notary has taken over his office."

Coralie left Aline in a rush. Uneasy, disturbed, she hailed a ligne, a taxi on a route that dropped her off at Mr. Hamel's office. A sign placed on the pediment above the metal doors leading to a small vestibule read:

OFFICE OF MR. MAURICE FLOREAL, ATTORNEY,

SUCCESSOR TO MR. HAMEL, ATTORNEY

Welcomed courteously by Mr. Maurice Floréal, an elegant young lawyer, Madame Nivel was able to take into account all of Aline's hypocrisy and cleverness. Mr. Floréal proved to her that her step-mother had managed to have the French Embassy deliver some papers to her stating that Coralie Santeuil Nivel, mother of Gratien Félix Nivel, minor, had been declared dead in Lille, in the Pas de Calais Department, following a bombing and that, as a result, it was necessary to establish a family council to manage the child's assets until he came of age. His uncle, Marceau Santeuil, had been named *legal guardian and trustee of the assets. Then, after several months, a public auction of the ten houses left to his wife and son by Gratien had taken place. Those buildings had been purchased at ridiculously low prices by a certain Anthony Rogival, a devotee of the Santeuils and a straw-man for Marceau Santeuil. Dismayed, Coralie couldn't get over the number of skillful tricks. She knew that Aline was capable of the worst schemes, but to have gone this far ... The young lawyer convinced her that it would be better to get along with her parents rather than begin a long, costly lawsuit that would perhaps only make her, and her son along with her, poorer and socially disreputable. Besides, how would she begin such a lawsuit without support and resources? Against whom would she bring her case? Against the mother of her brother, named her son's legal guardian? Against the wife of her father, named deputy guardian? What a lot of nastiness Aline would drag out in court! Worn out from surprise and indignation, Coralie felt Mr. Floréal gently take her hand while murmuring consoling words:*

"Rest assured, Madame, that I'll help you find an arrangement acceptable to your family."

His voice promised help and his gentle, dark eyes even more. Coralie was startled. Did she owe it to her beauty and her appearance as a touching victim to attract men's praise the moment she found herself in need? Did she only have her body as currency? And only her favors as her fortune? She stiffened and said:

"Thank you, Sir. Thank you for your frankness. I'll find out what needs to be done to defend myself and have my son back."

The young lawyer looked at her with the same compassionate tenderness, nodded his head dubiously, opened his mouth, swallowed, and finally uttered clearly:

"I wish you good luck, Madame."

She left and returned to the street. What was she going to do? She took another taxi and had herself driven to "Bord de Mer," to Félicien Santeuil's store, now F. Santeuil and Son. Marceau was seated at Félicien's large desk covered with green leather. The entire estab-

lishment seemed renovated, spruced up. The walls had been repainted with light colors; new display cases and counters were lined up in orderly fashion. A hardware department occupied one part of the spacious store where padlocks and faucets in an extensive, modern display were visible.

"Everything here breathes cleanliness," thought Coralie, "and with good reason."

She walked straight toward Marceau and extended a hand which he pretended not to see.

"Oh, there you are," was her younger brother's sole welcome.

"Oh yes, here I am, and I've been learning some surprising things. It seems that you, egged on by your mother of course, deprived Félix and me of our inheritance."

"And with the approval of our father, my dear. It was really necessary to protect your son from you."

"From me? From me?" repeated Coralie, staring at him.

"Yes, from you. The Free France group had you tracked for evidence of collaboration. Yes, my dear, even here, we knew that you were selling the secrets of your comrades in the Resistance to your German lover who transmitted them to the Gestapo. A nice job, whore and spy. It couldn't have been any better."

Crushed by shame and horror, Coralie opened wide her immense, terrified eyes. Marceau felt that he had the upper hand and tried again:

"The government of liberated France could have had you extradited, shot like Mata Hari, or guillotined like Doctor Petiot."

Marceau Santeuil was familiar with his older sister's fragile disposition. He knew that all he had to do was strike hard for her to break down. Aline had taught him often enough that Coralie was naturally *submissive and that she did not know how to resist for very long. Coralie stammered:*

"It's hateful, it's garbage ... garbage ...."

And she suddenly burst into tears. This is the moment Marceau had been waiting for to become more pleasant.

"Believe me, my dear Coralie, believe me. The best thing you can do for yourself is to have people forget about you and to make yourself inconspicuous. We'll pay you an allowance generous enough to enable you to live decently, and then, when the time comes, we'll turn all of the assets over to Féfé."

And since she was still sobbing, already subdued and accepting, he added patiently:

"Everything Mama, Papa, and I have done is for your own good and for Félix's, too. We all love you and, after all, we are your only relatives on this miserable earth."

Indifferently, he accompanied her to the office's threshold, then toward the store's exit. He continued to speak:

"Come to see your son tomorrow. He's the spitting image of Gratien. He's a smart, strong little fellow. You'll see. You'll be quite happy together. See you tomorrow, dear Cora."

By using Cora, the nickname that old Philo alone had given her when she was a child, he finished softening her up, nudging her still further into acceptance and renunciation.

She went out, feeling drawn, blinking her pale eyes in the hot ten-o'clock sun. It was not too late to go see Auguste Percier, the director of Gratien Nivel's enterprise to whom she had entrusted her late husband's business before leaving Haiti eight years ago. Only eight years of her life had passed, and already it seemed like more than a century. Then she had had husband, house, servants, car, jewels, friends, and protection. Now she was alone, having only the small sum loaned to her by the generous Lise Alphonsin to pay for her room and board. For how long would this faithful friend be able to finance her, since she was getting ready to open her own doctor's office? With what funds could she undertake prosecutions and sustain a lawsuit against her family? And then, a lawsuit against one's parents would require washing their dirty linen in public. She would be tainted forever and her only son besmirched forever. No, a patched-up agreement was better than a scandalous and costly lawsuit. She would have to brief the lawyers and without money to pay them for their services, they, too, would want to take it out on her. "After all, I'm in good health. I'm thirty-five years old, and I can work," she says to herself as she pushes open the glazed door closing off Auguste Percier's office.

Mr. Percier, always a little too pleasant and servile, sprang up to meet her. A good man, honest and timid, he would not hurt a flea, but he caved in under pressure.

He invited Coralie to sit down and took her two hands, saying several times in succession:

"Ah, Madame Nivel, Madame Nivel, if I had known … if I had known …."

"If you had known what, Mr. Percier?"

" … that you weren't dead, that you were alive …."

"What? What do you mean?"

"That I would never have accepted that the family council in charge of your under-age son make me do what I did."

"But what did you do?"

"Well, when we found out that you were dead, well when we believed that you were dead, the family council insisted that the company's assets be transferred to Gratien Félix Nivel, only son and unique heir of the deceased Nivel couple, oh! … that we believed dead, though only your husband had died. Well, I did it, and the revenue from the transactions is put each year in a trust which will revert to your son when he comes of age, and the interest ...."

Breathless from having talked so much, he stopped several times and wiped a stream of abundant sweat from his brow.

" ... the interest," resumed Coralie in a toneless voice.

"The interest is paid yearly to the family council, that is to say, to the child's guardians for his support, schooling, medical expenses, and for anything unexpected."

Overwhelmed, devastated, Coralie perceived the extent of the disaster. From the depths where she had sunk, she heard herself ask in a scarcely audible tone:

"So, what's left for me?"

"Alas, nothing, dear Madame. Absolutely nothing. Not a red cent."

A heavy silence established itself between the unimaginative, model employee and the ex-employer, presently ruined by her closest relatives.

"Can't you give me something each month? I am utterly broke."

"Alas, dear Madame," resumed Percier, in agony over this trying conversation, "at the very most, I could give you ever so discreetly, a small, monthly sum, let's say between eighty and one hundred dollars at the maximum, if I juggle the accounts."

Faced with Coralie's devastated appearance, Percier was on tenter-hooks.

"It's better that you don't come back here. You'll give me your address on the phone, and I'll send you faithfully each month in cash in a sealed letter what ... what I just promised you. But it's between us—strictly between us. You'll keep it secret, Madame. I risk losing my job ...."

Just as she was going to utter a reply, he added hurriedly:

"You understand, Madame. My job is important to me. At my age, it's not easy to find work in the business world, and I want to have an untroubled retirement."

"I understand you very well, Mr. Percier," replied Coralie, annoyed by the cowardice of the man who was shaking like a piece of gelatinous beef in its nasty, yellow grease.

"And thank you for what you thought you must do."

She took her purse, still containing fifty dollars loaned her by Lise, got a taxi, and went directly to the boarding house on Ducoste Avenue where she had been living since her return. The amount would undoubtedly last for another two weeks. She had prudently paid for her lodging and two daily meals for the next two months.

Lying on her bed under the ceiling fan that screeched above her like a carnival battle cry, she began to reflect.

Nothing. She no longer had anything. She had become poor. Aline had schemed magnificently and now had the profits from Nivel's export coffee business, the rent from the house at Pacot, and the returns from the eight other houses left by Gratien. Either officially or behind the scenes, the average income was the equivalent of a lifetime annuity. She, Coralie, who had sacrificed her youth to her old husband, who had embellished his last days, who had procured for him the greatest joy of his life by giving him a long-awaited son, no longer had anything at all.

In her heart of hearts, she already knew that she would accept any kind of arrangement Aline offered her. Anything rather than call her elderly father to court to testify for the other side. Anything rather than expose the disgraceful behavior of her father's wife and the depravity of her own life to a public greedy for scandal. Anything, even misery, rather than bringing out into the open the sordid, seamy side of the Santeuils' lives.

After all, she was just barely thirty-five, she was young and hardy, she was going to organize her life to get back on her feet again. She was going to work.

But how? Coralie Santeuil Nivel absolutely did not know how to do anything at all.

THE EIGHTH STATION

DECEMBER 31: CHAMPS DE MARS

3:00 P.M.

With legs weak from so much walking, Coralie finally arrived at the Champ de Mars. Shade at last! At last a peaceful corner where the reflection of the still burning hot December afternoon sun is filtered by the velvety shade of the trees which rustle in this spot behind the Pantheon Museum. The poor woman sits down at the base of the tall foliage in this public square, witness to so many uprisings, revolutions, carnivals, and other activities.

Coralie catches her breath for a moment and rests her head up against the trunk of a tree which gives off an unusual coolness. Not far from her, three street vendors, themselves looking for some rest, chat under the green canopy. Further ahead, the tall bamboos sing an unfamiliar, soothing chant.

Cora feels her thin, faded fabric purse. She still has four dollars in it. From now on, she fully intends to use public transportation to arrive at her next stop, the residence of Doctor Lise Alphonsin, Robert's adoptive mother, who has always been good to her and who will not refuse to loan her at least a part of the sum she will need for the next day. And then, perhaps Robert … While Félix …. In short, she is needy, broke, destitute. She is not entitled to be proud.

To be proud? And consequently of what, Lord? Coralie, what have you done with your life? Everybody can ask her this question. As you make your bed, so you must lie on it, and nobody cares about the downtrodden.

She is nothing more than a beggar, a pauper. The only difference is that she is aware that her fair skin and blue eyes, washed out from so much crying, make of her, without her even trying, a cheater, a social anomaly. *Yon bel milatrès konsa, e pi se pòv ou ye?* You are such a beautiful mulatto woman, and yet you are so poor? *A, se espre ou fè.* Ah, you're doing this on purpose. *Coralie, mnaman, ou fè espre!* My dear Coralie, it is entirely your own fault!

She listens to the words of the three vendors, or rather of two male and a female vendors of candies. The latter is complaining about hard times. Too much competition. You make the best money around the movie theaters. But for a woman, the tray is heavy, the strap pinching her shoulder cuts into her neck, and she is so tired, especially because she suffers from a displacement of the uterus. It feels good sitting in the shady coolness of this undergrowth for a short respite while waiting for the next show at the Paramount or at the Rex theaters. Her companions in misery comment and agree:

"Epi poukisa atò? Pou fe de twa goud benefis pa jou? And why is that? Just to make a few bucks a day? What can a full-grown man do with one or two bucks a day?"

"Sitou si ou gen madann ak pitit sou kont ou. Especially if you have a wife and children to take care of."

The first one goes even further:

"As for you, you have a wife who helps you. My wife died last year while in labor. Since then, it's a good Christian, *a vwazin ki okipe timoun yo pou mwen,* a neighbor, who takes care of my children for me. I send them to public school. They are making progress and are beginning to *teke nan franse a,* tackle French a little bit, but it's vacation time that worries me. During that time, our neighbor can't control them, especially my girl *ki se yon ti demwazèl ki fèk fòme,* the one who just entered puberty."

"A monchè ou lan ka ... ou lan ka ... Ah, my dear," resumes the woman with a sigh, "you're in trouble., *Mwen mwen, se katòzan mwen te genyen lè yon tonton m fè kadejak sou mwen e pi li gwòs mwen. Mwen fè pitit la mwen poko te gen kenzan.* As for me, I was only fourteen years old when my own uncle raped me. He got me pregnant, and I had a baby. I was not even fifteen. Thank God, the baby died two months later. Diarrhea carried him away. God saved me from having to care for him."

"Don't say that, my dear. It's not really deliverance. It's a tragedy. Who knows? This child could have been the one *ki ta leve ou atè a,* to lift you up out of poverty."

"Anyway, I had six children after the one that died, and I have yet to see when one of them will do something for me."

"And you husband, what does he do?"

"Ah, that man ... I've had children with three different fathers, *twa papa pitit,* and the one I'm living with right now *se yon machan fresco,* he is an ice-cone vendor. Only one of the kids is his. He does what he can, but he shouldn't be responsible for all of them. He's the one who gave me this little candy business so that I can see if I can make ends meet."

"It's better to make one or two bucks a day than nothing. *Se anyen anyen net ki ba bon.* The worst thing you can do is to make nothing, nothing at all!"

And the conversation unfolds in this way for a long time. "They are resigned to their fate," thinks Coralie. "They're not seeing the end of the tunnel of miseries. Someone, somewhere, has committed them to life without asking their opinion. They are destined to die poor and naked just as they have lived."

What if Coralie Santeuil, Coralie *Je Dajan,* Cora Silver Eyes, Cora *Janm Debwa,* Cora Wooden Leg, were to have just a small tray bringing her in two gourdes every day, with which she could at least eat on a regular basis? You can buy a big plate of rice with sauce, seasoned meat *ak berejenn,* meat with eggplant, cornmeal *ak afiba,* a dish made with cow udders, and greens with white rice for two gourdes in the street stalls, where homemade food is sold.

But Cora no longer has those two gourdes earned on a regular basis since her poor hands can no longer wash and iron, since she slipped from poverty to total misery.

The conversation between the three vendors continues softly, interspersed with long stretches of silence only disturbed from time to time by a long *tuipe,* a sonorous sigh of disgust or by a stream of saliva disappearing in the green grass.

The humming voices are muffled, gentle, and soothing, and Coralie falls asleep to their murmur.

She sleeps, worn out from fatigue and crushed from worry. She sleeps one hour ... two hours? She does not have a clue except that the light has changed during her nap, and it is already dark under the tall trees. When she finally wakes up, she is surprised to find in her bowl-shaped deformed hand, three candies, a roll of multicolored lifesavers, and a tiny box of raisins.

Which one of the vendors left her these modest provisions for her journey?

Which one of the three stole her purse?

NINE

The day after her meeting with Aline, then those with Mr. Floréal and Auguste Percier, Coralie decided to stifle her pride and finally go to meet her son at the Santeuils.

She made up her mind to see the child first, talk with him, and try to win him over before broaching serious discussions with Aline. After all, children love fairies and a pretty, very pretty mother who arrives out of the blue is bound to please a sensitive, dreamy, nine-year-old little fellow like Félix. The boy did not even know her from a photograph. She was going to make herself so beautiful that the child could do nothing but throw himself into the arms of his long lost mother.

In her well-stocked wardrobe, she chose a supple, light green crêpe dress with long, flowing panels whose color harmonized with a redhead's skin tones. She gathered her hair into a soft chignon resting on her slender neck. Wearing beige suede shoes, she selected a pair of leather gloves in the same shade, then put on a light-colored, broad-rimmed straw hat trimmed with small green roses adding a floral touch.

She gazed at herself in the large mirror of the sturdy armoire with antique glass that filled up a section of the wall. She smiled at herself in the mirror and thought she was irresistible with her light make-up, barely rouged checks, and discreetly colored ruby lips opening on a perfect set of teeth. What normal child would not be happy to have such a pretty mother to love in such a short time?

Coralie had seduced so many men; she had received from all of those who had approached her so many flattering compliments that the thought never crossed her mind that Félix might have been prepared by Aline to welcome her coldly. She crossed the garden of the family home with an assured pace and, light as a feather, climbed the six steps of the stairs laid out in a fan-shaped stone pattern at the end of the paved walk.

Aline, as stiff and difficult as usual, stood at the top of the steps. She held out her severe forehead to Coralie and said to her:

"Hello. Follow me. Félix has a temperature this morning. I'm making him stay in his room. He must have caught a nasty flu in school."

Coralie followed her stepmother, all the while examining her childhood home. She saw once again the big drawing room where the chairs were always protected by khaki slipcovers so that, according to Aline, "they wouldn't be spoiled." The same Turkish carpet, a little more worn in spots, covered the beautifully waxed, inlaid parquet floor. The odor of the beeswax polish caught her in the throat. Moved, she thought: "Even if I was unhappy in it, it is my house just the same." Behind Aline, she climbed effortlessly the rather steep staircase that led to the first floor.

Aline had settled Félix in the bedroom that had been his mother's. Her throat tightened at the sight: if nothing had changed elsewhere in her paternal home, here everything had been deliberately redone. The walls, once covered in beige paper with tiny flowers faded by time, had been cleaned up and painted with pale blue enamel. Some very contemporary, Swedish teak furniture had replaced her bed and armoire. The bed was a light-colored wood couch framed by bookshelves displaying a radio and a collection of miniature cars. A modern wardrobe housed clothes, and a polished chest-of-drawers held underwear. On the walls were some school pennants, and on the dresser was a small gilded trophy of a soccer player and a ball certifying Félix as a champion in one of the school's lower division competitions. A tall mirror was attached to the door of what was clearly a private bathroom.

This bathroom had been made out of a closed section of the large balcony. It was a modern bathroom with all of the latest conveniences for this child while she, Coralie, had had a hard time obtaining a pitcher and a wash-basin from Aline to wash herself. She had to take her soap and towel and go off every morning to splash in the cold water of the large reservoir adjoining the kitchen. There, shivering, chilled, she had to lather her body hastily, then plunge all at once into the greenish water shared with the frogs and their tadpoles. Aline had done things on a grand scale, and Félix must surely also have a shower and hot water.

All of these thoughts only took Coralie a second. She was already kneeling down close to the "cozy corner" and speaking softly to the sullen little boy whose cheeks and eyes revealed his feverish condition.

Coralie murmured:

"Félix, my little Féfé. It's me, your mama."

"Don't know you."

Aline intervened curtly:

"Félix, this is your mother who has come to see you. Come on. Make an effort. Give her a hug."

Coralie had to bend over the little face, and Félix's lips stretched out into a small, unwilling pout which felt to her like a burning iron.

"But he has a high fever," she says to Aline in order to keep herself pulled together.

And she pretended to examine the bedroom to keep Aline from seeing her tear-filled eyes.

"Yes, he often catches the flu. He gets his fragile throat and bronchial tubes from Gratien, but with the exception of flues and frequent colds, the child is in good health," says Aline.

Félix had been fidgeting in his bed for several minutes. Aline noticed him and said in a gentler tone:

"Féfé, do you need to pee? Get up and go to the toilet."

The irritable child grumbled:

"Don't want to pee in front of the lady."

"Come on, Félix. Don't be stubborn. Go and pee. This person isn't "the lady." She's your mother, Coralie. We've talked to you about her."

And she added sarcastically:

"She used to live in France, but she decided to come to see you in Haïti. So, you must be nice."

"Don't like her," murmurs Félix while getting up.

And Coralie realized then just how ugly her son was. He had the same features as Gratien Nivel, softened by the roundness of childhood. A large, round head, a face already puffy with fat, small, piglike eyes. This unpleasant face was not tempered by the great goodness which penetrated the features of the late Gratien Nivel. Shaped by Aline, Félix was already nasty and sneaky.

The little fellow got up to go to the bathroom, and Coralie saw that he had his father's shape. Short on his feet, his torso was too long, and his skinny arms were attached to a narrow chest and the erect shoulders of an asthmatic. Coralie was angry with herself for noticing that Félix, son of an old man, had inherited nothing from her. In short, her son was an ugly, unpleasant little gnome.

Horribly disappointed by the child's appearance and greeting, she inquired:

"And school? Is he doing well in school?"

"You didn't see the large size of his head and his ears? These are signs of intelligence, my dear. And Féfé se yon boul lespri, Féfé is a brain. Always at the head of his class, on the honor roll every month."

Coralie felt slightly relieved. If Félix had gotten Gratien's ugliness, he had likewise inherited his father's intelligence. While she, Coralie, had only done mediocre studies and had retained just the basics of ill-assorted knowledge that Gratien had tried to enrich her with during the last two years of their life together. But unfortunately,

Gratien died too soon to make her an educated woman. With her European stay, impeccable spoken French, visits to museums, concerts, theaters, and especially thanks to three years spent living with Klaus von Dieter, Coralie had acquired a superficial polish that could deceive others in a drawing room but would not stand up in the company of vre save, of true intellectuals.

She was thinking about all of these things when Félix came back from the bathroom. The child threw himself angrily on the bed, punched his pillow several times, and took a book by Edgar Rice Burroughs, the latest adventure of Tarzan, the ape-man, and immersed himself openly in his reading.

"And rude on top of everything else. An honest-to-goodness little bear," thought Coralie.

Aline's domineering voice rose:

"Féfé, put down your book and tell your mama good-bye before she leaves. Come on, Félix!"

The child obeyed reluctantly and got out of bed. It was eventually Coralie who placed a kiss on his burning forehead.

It was all over. This meeting in which she had placed so much hope was a total fiasco. Not for one minute had she felt any outburst of emotion or maternal feeling for this ugly, rude child. Nothing but sad indifference. For she realized that if she owed it to herself to love Félix, nothing about this child drew her to him. The mother and the son had met like strangers. They had not reunited.

Besides, the child was visibly under Aline's thumb, and he would remain there. It was Aline who had molded his heart and his mind for nine years. And even if she had initially wanted it, Coralie felt no real desire to recover her son's affection. No electric current had passed between Félix and herself. The spark had not ignited. Félix would remain indifferent and would never love her.

Too late. Once again and always too late. Nothing could fill the gap between her son and herself, a gap created by her absence at the moment the child's emotional sensitivity was developing. She had not fed him, rocked him, changed him. She had not laughed with him while bathing him. She had not given him any of those inexpensive toys that delight for a day and that children enjoy breaking. She had not told any of those bed time stories intended to make him sleepy, any of those tales that inhabit children's sleep with sweet dreams. She had known neither night-time tears that a mother's arms soothe nor the smiles of babbling awakenings. When he had cried during one of those child's nightmares, it was Aline who had rushed to rock him in her arms and calm him down. Coralie had known neither his first laugh, his first tooth, nor his first steps. Last year, he had his first communion, the important one, and it was not Coralie who brought him to and from the seminary's secondary school chapel. His first report cards had been signed by Aline or Marceau, for Coralie had just learned that her father had become an invalid five years ago.

It was only to hide her considerable disappointment that she said, almost in a whisper:

"And Papa, how is he?"

"He's not well. Not well. He has had two strokes, and he is completely paralyzed on the right side. On the left side, only his arm and hand still move. You saw him yesterday," responded Aline in her consistently unsympathetic voice.

Coralie mustered all of her strength in order to again face the sight of the paralytic who was asleep on the terrace in his wheelchair, his lifeless legs covered with a Scottish plaid blanket whose bright colors contrasted with Félicien's emaciated, gray face.

Upon seeing his daughter, the old man formed a distressing grin in the left corner of his mouth, and a joyful glimmer lit up his eye, danced there a moment, and disappeared as if it had been blown out from inside his body.

He stammered:

"Cora ... Coralie ...."

Then:

"You've come back ...."

"But Papa, I saw you yesterday."

"Yesterday, never ... well, maybe ..."

In tears, Coralie threw herself on her knees close to the wheelchair and covered her father's hands with moist kisses.

"Papa, dear Papa," she sobbed.

Félicien tried to continue:

"It's been a long time ...."

Then continued:

"You are very beautiful ...."

And that was all. His face recaptured its dismal immobility as if gripped by enormous suffering.

"Come along. Let's go. You are tiring him out," said Aline.

"Is he suffering a lot?" inquired Coralie who was doing her best to dab her tears in a batiste handkerchief. The initials K.D. with a crown over it reminded her that Klaus had given her his handkerchief to dry her tears and blow her nose like a little girl one day when she had felt overcome by her home-sickness for Haïti.

All of that seemed long ago in this house which had become foreign to her, confronting this helpless father, this unkind, grasping woman, this unbearable, grumbling child!

She heaved a long sigh and distanced herself slowly from the invalid as if she were watching for a new flash of recognition on that imperturbable face. But Félicien's mind had drifted far away again, far from everything, far from this insufficiently loved daughter whom he rediscovered too late.

Too late, always too late.

Coralie shook off the apathy that overtook her, and the profound despair that she felt gave her the energy to confront Aline, who murmured:

"You know he's not all there."

"Was he all there when you and Marceau contrived to extort my holdings and to deprive Féfé of his inheritance?"

"You mean in order to protect your son's inheritance. Your notorious misconduct, your unpleasant dealings with the post-war French government, the scandal about your morals, everything about you predicted that you would squander all of your money with your numerous lovers before Féfé would come of age."

"But there is justice. I will defend myself, and I will force you to restore my estate."

"Ah, you really think so? What do you intend to do without re-sources, without friends, my dear? Nan peyi isit, tout bagay se kòb ak relasyon. Ou pa gen ni yon, ni lòt. In this country, everything is money and connections. You have neither. Go ahead and sue, my dear. Do it. We will expose everything, Coralie, everything. And, in any case, we will have you declared incapable of managing your own affairs, and we will prove that a woman who leads an immoral life is incapable of assuming moral responsibility and the education of a child. All you will do is lose your son a second time."

Then she added insidiously:

"Whereas if you show that you are reasonable ...."

"Reasonable?"

"Yes, if you consent to leaving things as they are, if you give up the idea of a costly, scandalous trial, Marceau and I are inclined to pay you a comfortable allowance and let you visit your son once each month. It wouldn't be good for him to see you too often."

"Couldn't I go out with him sometimes? Take him for a walk?"

Coralie was already giving in. Her small amount of natural combativeness was already yielding to Aline's unbending will.

Aline said to her very firmly:

"No, the visits will take place here in my presence. You will not be able to go out with Féfé. Coralie, you aren't going to change. The parade of your lovers could give Félix health problems and set an excessively bad example. For the sake of Féfé's stability, he must remain under our absolute control."

Defeated by Aline's resolve, Coralie murmured:

"You have taken everything from me. Snatched everything."

"It's for your son's own good that we will shelter him from your dissolute life. It's for his own good, too, that we have sheltered his fortune from your wasteful spending and your lax conduct. Consider yourself fortunate, Coralie, to still have enough left to live on thanks to our prudent wisdom. You are still lucky, Coralie, very lucky."

"Yes, lucky enough to lose everything," murmured Coralie.

"I'll send you a check each month through Mr. Floréal that you can pick up in his office. As you can well imagine, you needn't bother to come back here often. Too frequent visits from you will upset Félix and disturb your father. I'll let you know the stipulated days. Once each month. No more."

"I'll never come back, Never again."

"As you wish, my dear. You've always been stubborn. The lawyer will therefore hand you your check."

"For how much?"

"I'll inform you. You won't be disappointed. I know how to do things properly. And as for your son's money, it has been sensibly invested, and Marceau is aware of how to make it bear interest. And all of it will be given back to him when he comes of age so that the concerns of a mother ...."

Aline stopped and added with a little, sarcastic sneer:

... of an intermittent mother, let's say, will be completely appeased."

On the walk bordered with flowering stragornias, Coralie, left, bewildered. She said good-bye to all of her memories, her ties, the rosebush she loved, her father, her son, and the old, wooden villa with its decorative fretwork that was for her, in spite of everything, her home.

Before her, the future. But what future for Coralie, the one who had been exiled, banished, and disinherited?

THE NINTH STATION

DECEMBER 31: BOIS VERNA, AVENUE DU TRAVAIL

5:00 P.M.

Coralie does not have any more money to catch the taxi that would take her to Bois Verna, or more precisely to Avenue du Travail where Lise Alphonsin and Robert live. She is desperate, but she doesn't blame whoever relieved her of her scanty savings. They must have thought she was less poor than they because, in spite of her physical condition, she has the appearance of a former *gwo moun*, a member of the wealthy class.

Before starting out again, she massages her sore feet. Oh, a strap has snapped, freeing her left toe where she suffers from a big, painful corn. She has been dragging this *zòbòy*, a large corn on her big toe for many years. Now it is exposed. She is relieved. The strap eating into her foot had tortured her since morning. It is not very pretty. The shoes are a bit too tight for feet no longer accustomed to narrow shoes. The plastic basket weave has left a pattern of square cushions of skin where blood has accumulated. Now her feet are marked with strange little bulging pink and grey squares. With her only good hand, she rubs her sensitive feet tenderly for a long time and laboriously puts her shoes back on.

And she sets out again along Avenue Magny, then Lamartinière Avenue. She eventually takes Ruelle Vilmenay, a lane which winds its way to Avenue du Travail. She pushes open the forged iron gate closing off the countyard of the superb gingerbread residence that Lise Alphonsin is spending her life restoring and improving. There is nothing but good taste, art, discreet silence, and peace here.

She rings the doorbell. An impeccably dressed servant in a rose gingham uniform, her hair tucked in a white handkerchief, her smiling face framed by two large Creole earrings, appears.

"May heaven protect the pretty girl from temptations," thinks Cora. The servant knows Coralie, who has come to see Lise and Robert now and then.

"Oh, hello, Madame Coralie. *Doktè a pa la non.* The Doctor is not here."

"*Ki lè lap rantre?* When is she going to come back?"

"It will be awhile. *Se Sendomeng lale pase fèt yo.* She went to the Dominican Republic for the holidays. Not necessarily for the holidays, but she was invited to a seminar on children so she's taking advantage of that to have a few days vacation."

So, this hope in turn falls through. Lise is absent, out of the country, far away, inaccessible.

"And Mr. Robert?"

"Mr. Robert doesn't live here anymore with the doctor. He rented his own place four months ago, no six months ago. He left last June. I remember because school was not out yet."

"And where does he live now?"

"Well, in Pétion-Ville in the Mòn Ekil area. He rented a really big, beautiful house there."

"But it's not something between him and … his mother?"

It is really difficult for Cora to pronounce those words "*manman li,*" his mother, when talking about Lise and Robert. Each time it is as if she were again abandoning the laughing, little boy who called her "Tatie" all over again.

"Oh no, but *se jèn gason, ou komprann,* he's a young man, you understand. *Li pa marye.* He's not married. *Li gen kòb nan men ni, li bezwen libète li pou viv alèz.* He's got money, so he needs freedom so he can live an easy life. But he comes to see Doctor Lise from time to time, and he calls her every evening on the phone."

"Ah …," sighs Coralie, who adds:

"Eske mwen pa kapab fè yon ti chita epi eske ou ka banm yon vè dlo? Can I sit down for a while, and also can you please give me a glass of water?"

"Oh, Madame Coralie, *chita, chita ou tout tan ouv le epi map ba ou youn bon ti ju zoranj, m pral fè l pou ou kounye a.* Go ahead and sit down. Sit down for as long as you want. And I'm going to give you a nice glass of orange juice! I'm going to make it for you right now."

And the servant withdraws. Cora settles down in a soft, fawn-colored leather armchair. She lets her clear eyes, which mist over, wander around: rich, silky, brocade drapes, leather furniture shining in the shadowy light, a carpet with a light background and dark arabesques, and paintings by well-known Haitian artists: over there a Lazard, here a Desruisseaux, opposite her a Cédor. A large, full-length standing mirror is framed by two bronze candalabra, adding an antique note to this elegant, modern interior.

Several beautifully bound books decorate a set of shelves housing a television set and a stereo. Although genuinely luxurious, it is an unpretentious room in which one feels deep peace, the presence of an intense cultural life, and considerable, undisturbed well-being. And Coralie catches herself dreaming about what her life might have been like if she had followed Lise's example: serious studies, an ideal of dedication to children's welfare, motherhood fulfilled through Robert's adoption, an oasis ….

When the servant comes back with the cool, sweetened orange juice, Coralie, the passer-by, has fled into the mauve twilight descending on the festive city.

TEN

Coralie went back to "La Belle Quarteronne," the boarding house where she was staying. She spent two or three days unable to recover from her meeting with her son, Marceau's cynical attitude, Aline's wickedness, and her father's physical deterioration.

Everything around her was crumbling. She was still fortunate that they would not let her die of hunger. How much was Aline going to give her to provide for her basic needs? She did not have any idea. Her depression was too great for a hundred dollars to make any difference. As a matter of fact, Coralie never had to keep track of money in her life and did not know its value. Above all, never having learned any trade, any profession, she was unaware of how hard it was to earn it and how quickly it melted in a hot, tropical sun.

Coralie remained in a state of profound depression for two or three weeks spending long hours stretched out on her bed or on a chaise longue on her small balcony, chain-smoking cigarettes whose butts she crushed before finishing them.

Where to go? Who to see? What to do? She called Auguste Percier and gave him her address and spoke briefly to Marceau's secretary to give it to him as well. She called Mr. Floréal to ask him to contact her stepmother and request that he be so kind also as to attend to receiving the money that Aline planned to allocate to her each month. The lawyer responded in a purring voice that he would be delighted to come himself to bring her this "alimony" that stingy Aline granted her stepdaughter. In her heart of hearts, Madame Santeuil knew that Coralie had the law on her side, and she feared the lawsuit that a more energetic person would not have failed to bring against her. So she decided to send the young woman four hundred dollars a month, the equivalent of the rent from one of the buildings extorted from Coralie. Four hundred dollars in the era immediately following the war was a fortune, and Aline would not have offered Coralie so much had she suspected that Auguste

Percier, for his part, was giving her another hundred dollars or so monthly. At that time, a State cabinet member scarcely earned more.

As soon as she received those first two installments, Coralie, who did not know how to calculate, believed that she had become almost as rich as she had been when Gratien was alive.

She prudently paid three months rent to her landlady who provided room and board for only one hundred dollars a month. Then, relieved of this concern, she made arrangements to renew her wardrobe. The clothes brought from France (with the exception of several extremely beautiful evening gowns given her by Klaus Von Dieter, and besides unwearable in Haiti), were outmoded fashions dating from the late thirties that she needed to replace, so she gave them to the two maids at the boarding house. She was going to deck herself out in the latest fashions all over again. She needed to buy herself those splendid, maxi skirts floating at the ankles, full as the petal skirts launched by Christian Dior to console European women for having gone so long without fabric. As soon as possible, she needed to replace those appalling platform soles made out of cork or wood that had replaced heels during the sad years of the occupation of France.

Get rid of the old and quickly embrace the good life! With this regimen, after a week or two, Coralie found herself without a cent.

How was she going to balance her budget at the end of the month if money trickled away so quickly? She already had debts and had to set money aside for the manicurist, the pedicurist, the hairdresser. She had given a batch of fabric to an excellent seamstress recommended by her landlady and who, even though she was not too expensive, required adequate payment for her work. Coralie realized that her allowance of five or six hundred dollars would not go very far if she did not augment it with some other source.

Working was more easily said than done. Intelligent but lazy, Coralie became aware that she had led a life of luxury, the life of a mindless doll that needed now to be brought down to earth in order to find a suitable job. Unfortunately, she did not have many talents.

Jabbering a little Spanish and Italian picked up during her travels, she thought she could apply at the travel agency "Forteresse," the first of its kind in Haïti. Having made herself exceptionally beautiful and elegant for the interview, the owner was pleased with her and seemed on the verge of hiring her when, in response to a specific question from her interviewer, she was obliged to say that she did not understand or speak a word of English. Coralie tried to get herself out of this fix by simpering and saying that she had never had the opportunity to go to England or the United States because of the war that had trapped her in France, but that she was going to study it and that, after all, it was no more difficult to learn English than any other language.

But the owner was inflexible. Only the American tourist interests Haitian travel agencies, and English was indispensable for the position of receptionist she was applying for. The gentleman from "Forteresse" wanted a "social attachée" totally fluent in American English, and he showed her to the door with a resolute politeness accompanied by a categorical refusal. He invited her to come back in several months after she learned how to speak English fluently, and then he would see.

It was the same story in all of the other deluxe stores where she applied as a saleswoman. Certain businesses such as Auxila hired only men; other owners were uncomfortable when they saw such a well-dressed woman, a former client, coming to apply for a job. It had not crossed Coralie's mind that she should have worn a simple, conservative dress when asking for employment. Wanting to make a good impression, she emphasized her elegance, her distinguished bearing, her speech which caused the other employees to say:

"Oh, oh, sa li ye la a, *what's happening here?* Kote fanm blanch sa a sòti? Sal konprann? *Where does this white woman come from? Who does she think she is?" or other similar compliments.*

Eventually understanding that these excessively luxurious outfits were being held against her, Coralie resigned herself to wearing plain black pumps, a navy blue skirt, and a white blouse. She disciplined her thick, red hair into a severe chignon and was finally hired at "Le Chandelier," a restaurant on the Rue Bonne Espérance in a neighborhood with plenty of clients. The business was successful because it

*provided warm dishes, sandwiches, and all kinds of drinks to the
Bord de Mer employers and employees who worked more than
eight-hours, and even longer during the end-of-the-year holiday
season.*

*Coralie was mortified to wear the white apron and the starched
waitress cap. The only good thing was that no one knew her in that
environment. She had been fortunate to live in a closed social circle
during her time with Gratien, and besides, the restaurants in the
lower part of the city had as their customers only men who, for the
most part, had never known Madame Gratien Nivel in her hours of
glory and took her for a foreigner.*

*She suffered martyrdom. The poor woman burned herself in the
kitchen picking up dishes and serving coffee. Removing the cap from
a bottle of cola or beer was a difficult process for her, and she often
broke the neck of the bottle, a loss for the restaurant. Because she
was pretty, polite, and pleasant, they withdrew her from serving in
the dining room to a position behind the counter preparing sandwiches and drinks. The owner was not unkind and sincerely wanted
to retain the poor girl she had initiated to the "basics of proper food
service:" know how to give the customer the least food for the most
money.*

*So all day long, others heard the owner, who dominated the cash
register, shouting to Madame Nivel:*

"Coralie, ou mete twòp moutad nan sandwich la, *you put too much
mustard on the sandwich.*"

"Coralie, se yon tigout sòs tomat wi pou mete sou ambègè a, *you put
just a little dash of tomato sauce on the hamburger ....*"

"My dear, one onion for six sandwiches. Don't waste it ...."

"Cora, my dear, when you're making a malted milk, you use only
yon ti kiyè, *one small spoonful of malt in the machine, and then you
make it foam.*"

In short, Coralie, used to excessive generosity and money, was ruining the restaurant. So, six months later, the down-to-earth owner, a woman Coralie intimidated by her behavior and her manner, politely let her go. The owner had vaguely sensed that Coralie te gwo moun, that she was from a privileged background, amd that she had been driven behind her counter by life's ups and downs, by what she called lavi bese leve.

If Coralie at least had managed to earn enough to pay for some secretarial courses and to learn English, she would have been able to secure a lucrative and, from her point of view, less disgraceful position. Wiping the table with a damp cloth in front of two or three intoxicated gentlemen and asking "And for the gentlemen, what will it be?" just the way she had seen it done in Paris, Madame Nivel, née Sauteuil, intimidated the customer because in Haiti the waitress— most often, a waiter—does not suggest anything. He stands in front of the customer and does not speak, waiting until the customer wishes to speak to him.

Coralie, who had never had to do anything but ring to have what she needed to feed herself brought from the pantry, was buttering sandwiches. Even now at the boarding house, she was pampered by the maids to whom she had generously given her old dresses and shoes from Paris.

Model-like with her tall, slim body, she could have shown dresses if, at the time, there had been ready-to-wear or high fashion houses in Port-au-Prince. Perhaps she could teach grade school, but her pale pointu, her Parisian French tone would not fool a principal with proper training for very long. The principal would soon recognize that her superficial knowledge was not grounded in any pedagogical or methodological concept.

She looked at her hands that did not know how to do anything and was horrified to see that, in several weeks, her tapered fingers were swollen and red from washing-up in the restaurant's hot or cold water; that her nails were broken and dull; that here and there still appeared the traces of the blisters resulting from having burned herself. Even on her forearm, pulling back her whitened skin, she discovered to her horror a small scab that was drying. What to do?

Looking at the calendar, she noticed that it was only the thirtieth of the month. Ordinarily, the allowance that Aline granted her was given to her only on the fifth or sixth of the following month by Mr. Floréal. He came to the boarding house on a regular basis in the evening to bring her this money and occasionally sat down at a table with her to have a coffee, a beer, or smoke a cigaret.

She found him handsome, gentle, elegant. His resonant voice had soft, tender inflections, and his dark, velvety eyes lingered discreetly on Coralie's low-necked dress. But since the day she went to see him at his office, he had not dared take her hand again and was satisfied to gaze at her intently with his adoring eyes.

"Today is the thirtieth. I am completely out of money. I have to pay the landlady at "La Belle Quarteronne," and I can't wait for Percier either who does not pay me until the fifteenth of the month. Well, I'm going to visit Mr. Floréal. Perhaps, by chance, Aline has already forwarded my check to him."

She looked at her hands. What was the young laywer going to think of her? The genuine hands of a servant. She filed and repaired her nails, massaged her fingers and palms with a moisturizing cream, but nothing helped: her hands spoke clearly about the servile and mortifying tasks she had been compelled to perform.

"Nonsense! Too bad! I'll wear gloves," she says, slipping into the shower.

Then she selected a long-sleeved dress to hide the burn marring her right arm. The white chiffon with the pink polka dots of her airy dress danced about her as she got out of the taxi at Mr. Floréal's office. He was standing in the clerks' front office, and he was giving instructions to the one who was recopying the draft of a contract. Lifting his head, he looked at her, cool and light, a veritable springtime breeze, and stammered:

"You … you!"

And he took her hand to lead her into his office, sparingly but luxuriously furnished. Black leather sofa and chairs, beige carpet, floral vases, and shiny, brass objects. On the wall, an oil painting by Savain and a watercolor by Ramponneau added an artistic note to this rich interior. Coralie said softly to herself: "Good taste ... and wealth."

Mr. Floréal approached her, took her hand in its white kid glove, and murmured:

"To what do I owe the honor of your visit, dear Madame Nivel?"

"You needn't be so polite. Just call me Coralie."

"Dear Coralie, you make me so happy. What can I do to please you? Why didn't you let me know you were coming? I could have prepared some refreshments."

"This is a spontaneous visit, Maurice. You will give me permission to call you by your fist name, too, won't you, Maurice? I was in your neighborhood running some errands, and I thought I would just drop in to say hello."

Choking with delight, he stammered:

"Coralie ... Coralie, you know that you've really made me happy. Wait, the day is almost finished. Let me send my office workers home. You'll wait a few minutes; I still have to sign some papers, and I'll take you to dinner at the "Wiener Hof." It's not too far from your boarding house, and we can talk there."

Floréal left the room for a moment to give some orders. Coralie heard the noise of drawers being closed, typewriters locked and covered, chairs pushed and put back in position, papers hastily gathered. Then three voices said in unison:

"Good-bye, Sir. We'll see you on Monday."

"Until Monday." Coralie had not thought about it being Friday afternoon and that everything closed for two days.

"Rats. He will not have received the money, and I'll have to wait until Monday."

But Maurice Floréal was already coming back towards Coralie and taking her hands.

"Say, say, Coralie, that you're not here by accident, but that you came to see me on purpose because you felt that I have loved you madly since the first day I saw you, that you have understood that seeing you once each month to give you Madame Santeuil's check was Tantalus' torment for me. Say that you knew that. Say it, darling, say it."

Coralie was satisfied to say with a sigh,

"Maurice ...."

"Oh, I love you, I love you, I desire you, I want you."

"Not here, Maurice. Not now. This is all too sudden. Later."

"No, here. We are alone, my love, and it is killing me to wait. Come on. I adore you. Come on. Be mine, now. I want you."

Coralie pretended to resist all the while latching herself on to Floréal's neck. Their lips united in a passionate kiss that made the lawyer moan.

"Cora, Cora, my Cora," he said in a voice which desire made hoarse.

And he threw her on the sofa where she let him penetrate her, thinking coldly that, from now on, she would have no trouble paying her bills at the end of the month.

THE TENTH STATION

DECEMBER 31: BOURDON

6:00 P.M.

Consumed with weariness, her legs shaking, Coralie keeps to the side of the road that goes from Bourdon to the Hôtel St. Christophe. There, on the right, almost at the beginning of the avenue, is the third of the wealthy residences bordering the lane. A tall fence with a colorful hedge running along the outside surrounds a structure made out of building stones and concrete whose balcony juts northward like the wing of a supersonic jet.

Cora rings at the gate. An electric bell sounds inside. A well-trained, obsequious butler appears at the fence. His body stiffens, and he almost pinches his nose. Who is this dowdy scarecrow who dares to ask to see Madame Rose Leblanc?

He answered that he is not sure Madame is in.

The poor woman insists:

"Go check for me. Tell her *se yon vye zanmi li Coralie ki bezwen wè li,* it's an old friend, Coralie who needs to see her."

The butler puts on the most haughty look. He is thinking to himself:

"Madame's friend … hum … See, I don't believe that for a minute." But trained to be obedient, he goes to announce the visitor, "*Min yon moun ki vin chache yon zetrenn,* somebody has come to look for a New Year's gift."

But he withdraws, thinking to himself:

"You never know about Madame's family members. *Milat sa yo si tan dwòl.* Those mulattos are so strange. *Ou pa janm fin konn zafè yo.* You can never really know what they're up to."

He comes back several moments later with visible repugnance to admit Coralie.

"Don't go through here. This is the reception room."

He does not dare say to her:

"With your filthy feet, you'll get the carpet dirty." And besides, it is New Year's Eve and the Leblancs are having guests. Everything is topsy-turvy.

"Go through here instead. Madame is by the pool."

Rose Darcey Leblanc sits enthroned on a white cane chaise-longue decorated with pink plastic cushions. Out of the coquetry of a child spoiled by life comes Rose's desire to surround herself entirely with pink decors. Her bedroom has pink curtains, a pink bedspread, a pink carpet, and her bathroom is a daintily furnished space where the pink tile matches the toilet, the bathtub, and the towels. The tall mirrors on the walls reflect Rose's impeccable silhouette. By means of massages, creams, masks, and exercise, she has kept the figure she had when she was thirty. Not wanting to add weight to this silhouette, she consented to having a child, but only one, a son who is presently a distinguished engineer and currently constructing a very expensive apartment complex.

Rose is proud of this son, but she is happy that Luc, after being married ten years, has no children. She, Rose Darcey, cannot image herself surrounded by a swarm of noisy brats calling her "grandmother." What a horror!

Wearing a pink linen beach outfit, her gray hair carefully dyed a fiery auburn, she is stretched out, her two hands in the air. Wads of toilet paper separate her toes shining with the pearly-pink nail polish she loves. Her manicurist-pedicurist left just minutes ago. While waiting for the polish to dry, she has at least ten minutes to devote to poor Coralie. A cordless telephone, within arms reach, is on the garden table covered by a large, pink umbrella whose shade adds yet another layer to the already heavily made-up mistress of the house.

She seems at least twenty years younger than her age. Good-hearted by nature though indifferent, she is superficial, frivolous, idle. An insular bird-brain in a pin-up's body.

Upon seeing the limping invalid who makes her way towards her chair, her hip dislocated, she exclaims:

"My dear Cora, how you have aged! *Sak rive ou konsa?*" What happened to you?"

"Lavi bat mwen anpil wi, Rose. I've taken a beating from life, Rose."

"Oh, my poor darling! Here I am jabbering away, and I'm not asking you if you want something to drink. What can I offer you? A cocktail, a Martini, a Manhattan or a Bloody Mary?"

Coralie thinks she is dreaming. Is it possible that Rose does not realize what her situation is like and that she is offering her these destructive drinks capable of damaging her already ruined stomach?

She sucked away the little candies from the Champ de Mars ages ago, all during the long journey. She left Lise's home without being able to drink the fruit juice that would have quenched her thirst and strengthened her a bit.

And in a voice made toneless from distress, she hears herself asking:

"If I could have a glass of milk ...."

"Wap bwè lèt la blanch konsa? Are you going to drink it plain? But still, Cora ... pure milk like that without either malt or chocolate ... Just a minute, I'm going to have a milk shake with chocolate ice cream made for you, like the ones you used to like."

And she rings the small bronze bell within reach of her right hand whose nails she examines as they go by. Soon they will be dry, and she will be able to attend to the house in preparation for the midnight supper on the Feast of St. Sylvester. It will be so much fun. She has planned some parlor games and entertaining gifts for the fifteen select guests coming to dinner at about eleven o'clock.

At about two or three in the morning they will finish their party at the Bamboula Club to the sounds of the Méridien Orchestra, especially fashionable these days.

Impatient, she rings again. The ever contemptuous butler appears, practically staring at the famished-looking visitor from head to foot.

"Hubert, *fè yon milkshake pou zanmi mwen ak de boul chokola ladan,* make a milkshake for my friend with two scoops of chocolate ice cream in it. And then also go to the *patisri* boxes which "Villa Mara" just brought in and prepare a plate for her ... you know ... a small selection of appetizers."

The disdainful flunky withdraws. "Why is Madame wasting her time *ak epav san zave saa,* with that no-good bitch, an old lady so ugly, so dirty? Besides, when those red-skinned people are dirty, they are worse than blacks."

Half an hour slips away before he comes back with the cold, frothy drink and a small plate the size of a saucer containing two pastry horns, three patties, a little tart with ham, and another with smoked fish and hard-boiled egg. Coralie eats with little bites trying to make this child's portion last. She would die rather than ask for anything else. She does her best to seem interested in Rose's jabbering, incessantly talking about Félix, her godson, and about his wife, Solanges, the center of gossip because of her affair with the handsome Syrian, Hassim Hafez, the darling of wealthy women. Rose chatters non-stop, laughs, asks and answers questions by herself. She has welcomed Coralie without noticing her anxious looks, without asking her even once the real reason for her visit.

After all, Cora has had her misfortunes, but Rose is her intimate friend. She baptized her son, and it is perfectly normal that she come to see her from time to time, but not too often just the same given the state of physical deterioration of the poor woman whose past as a former prostitute does not make her a desirable acquaintance. Fortunately, she always comes at the times when Henri Leblanc is not there. But her visits mustn't become too frequent, or prolonged, like today.

Rose talks and talks. She relates all of the latest gossip, and Coralie, who slowly relishes her chocolate milk shake, feels herself overcome with a pleasant lethargy.

Suddenly the telephone rings, and Rose grasps the phone with two cautious fingers.

"Hello. Yes? It's you, Marylise? Yes, what is going on?" she says, with her high pitched, piping voice.

"A catastrophe, my dear. A veritable catastrophe. I had promised to bring you some leaf lettuce this evening to garnish the platters, but I found, or rather my cook found nothing but head lettuce!"

Rose Leblanc lifted her horrified eyes to the heavens.

"Head lettuce! Oh no. As you know, my turkey is too beautiful, and my ham, a marvel. Oh no. Without leaf lettuce, the platters won't look like anything."

"So what are we going to do?"

"I'll meet you in no time by car, and we'll rush off to Kenscoff. Damned if we can't manage to get some leaf lettuce from the late vendors."

"That's an excellent idea. It's so important!"

"Head lettuce is so vulgar! *Se bagay moun òdinè.* That's what ordinary people eat. I'll be there shortly. *Mwen sou ou touswit.* I'll be there right away. I have a guest who is leaving now. See you soon. Ciao!"

Coralie understood the indirect summons. It is time for her to leave. And she hears herself say, in the tone of a woman of the world who has visited an equal:

"Thank you very much, Rose, for your delightful welcome, this delicious snack. I had come by to wish you Happy New Year."

"Thank you, Cora, and Happy New Year, too. I hope that you'll soon regain your health."

What a relief! The burdensome visitor is gone. Quickly, into the car and off to Kenscoff! Coralie had no success in capturing the actual attention of this whirling weathervane. Not an ounce of genuine interest. A mixture of trifles and wind!

How to express her moral and financial distress to this feather-brain whose car just passed her like a whirl-wind without even recognizing her?

ELEVEN

Coralie settled into her liaison with the young lawyer the way she did everything else, effortlessly, and without thinking too much about her future.

This tendency in her nature made her a mistress who was easy to please, provided that her lover defrayed the cost of clothing and beauty products, that he gave her flowers and perfumes, and, above all, that he took her out from time to time to the expensive, fashionable restaurants and ballrooms.

Soon a routine established itself in their relationship. She did not need to go to his office. At la Mer Frappée, Maurice had a bachelor pad where he took her two or three times a week depending on the leisure time afforded by his work. Sometimes, it was a weekend at Kenscoff, at Furcy, or in a beach hotel where they spent the better part of their time shut up in their bedroom, not venturing out on the deserted beach until nightfall.

Gradually, as their liaison took shape, Coralie got to know Maurice Floréal. The only son of a mother widowed early on, Maurice was very attached to this woman who dominated him completely.

He was still a bachelor at thirty-seven because none of the young women he had associated with were able to find favor in the dowager's eyes. This one was too thin and had fragile health; she would not give him sturdy children. That one was too pretty; she would certainly be unfaithful. That other one was flirtatious, extravagant; she would ruin him in record time. That last one was as silly as a goose and would harm his career. In short, bit by bit, Maurice became twenty-five, thirty, thirty-five years old without ever having met the rare pearl sought by his mother, who continued to treat him like a little boy.

After his studies to become a lawyer and a notary, she had bought him the practice established by Mr. Hamel, who wanted to retire after two benign heart attacks sent him a warning signal. Madame Mother had paid the full price for this well-established practice and had allowed Maurice to transform the office to make it more modern and attractive.

Maurice Floréal earned a very ample living staying with his mother in their big beautiful house and didn't worry about tomorrow, hoping that heaven would some day send him the perfect young girl who would satisfy his beloved mother's wishes.

A young girl, an authentic one, a virgin. Not one of those shameless little creatures who get themselves aroused at a dance or at the movies and go almost all the way with their boyfriends, not a half-virgin, but a young girl coming straight from a convent, closely supervised by Papa-Mama and others, who would leave home to go to the altar with a white veil and a crown of orange blossoms, and that he would deflower on the wedding night carefully keeping the white nightgown, soiled with the blood of the pure, sacrificial lamb, for the two mothers-in-law's inspection.

Otherwise, no marriage, and Coralie had immediately gotten the message. After several attempts to discuss the question, she had definitively understood that Maurice Floréal, as taken as he was with her, would never marry her. Besides, with her lukewarm feelings for the young lawyer, she really did not want to get married. She was enjoying a calm, stable, secure liaison.

She had everything she wanted. The two allowances arrived regularly and fell into her account like autumn leaves while Maurice assumed all of her other personal expenditures without hesitation.

As lazy as a lout, she felt just fine loafing in bed, smoking the Pall Malls or Winstons she preferred. A late riser, she read some illustrated novel or flipped through a beauty or fashion magazine. With the exception of Lise Alphonsin and Rose Darcey, she didn't see anyone. She went to the Champ de Mars, to the Rex or Paramount movie theaters on the evenings when she did not go out with Maurice, and afterwards she fell asleep peacefully. Coralie was well suited to her status as a kept woman, and basically, she did not love Maurice enough to want to share every moment of his life or to take care of his house, his food, and horror of horrors, his underwear and his socks. Oh, no. She would one hundred times rather remain a pampered mistress than become a housewife in a middle-class home.

With Maurice, who made love well and who satisfied her honorably, she readily imitated the behavior of a passionate lover. Some movements and some moans at just the right time were sufficient to prove to the young lawyer that he was sincerely loved.

And this lasted three years. Three years of unruffled happiness without any big outbursts of feeling on Coralie's part, without any wild, passionate acts on Maurice's part. And that could have continued another ten or fifteen years if Madame Floréal had not noticed that her son was approaching his fortieth birthday and that it was time for him to settle down, find a legitimate wife, and beget some little Floréals intended to make their future grandmother extremely happy.

With this in mind, she inquired about young women corresponding to her ideal and discovered the priceless daughter in law in Jacqueline Dubourg, the eldest daughter in a brood of five children belonging to some Cap Haïtien business people who had become wealthy in the sisal trade. Jacqueline was twenty-two, rather pretty, pious, even religious. She had never in her life had the slightest little affair and only left home chaperoned by her mother or her unmarried aunts who watched carefully over her virtue. All of the information was verified, reverified, and confirmed by some acquaintances from Cap Haïtien who, without exception, agreed in singing Jacqueline Dubourg's praises to Madame Floréal.

Then Madame Floréal began a conversation with her son:

"Maurice, you'll be forty next March."

"Yes, Mama."

"So, you're going to leave your mistress, that Madame Nivel, with whom you've been infatuated for three years."

"What, Mama … You knew?"

"Of course I knew. How could my good informants have left me in the dark about such a public liaison?"

"And you let me …."

"Of course, I let you carry on. A young, vigorous, unmarried man needs an outlet. He needs to sow his wild oats. And then, your fastidious dress, your costly perfumes, your nocturnal outings, your "working" weekends, or so you said, made me suspicious without my friends' tittle-tattle, my son. Your old mother isn't as stupid as she seems."

"Oh, Mama, you, stupid, come on …."

"Good. Now listen. I've unearthed the ideal young woman. I have excellent information about her, and I've seen her picture. She is exquisite, perfect from every point of view, and you'll be engaged immediately, and you'll be married in three months. Is that clear?"

"Yes, Mama."

"So, it is all over with Madame Nivel. Koupe m sa, put an instant end to it. A woman who has been fooling around before, during, and after her marriage will understand that a man of honor wouldn't dream of marrying her."

"We've never considered marriage, Mama. Never. I assure you."

"So much the better. The break will be all the easier. You'll give her a nice good-bye present, and that will be that."

"Yes, Mama."

"Do what needs to be done this very evening, because we're leaving for the Cap Saturday to ask Jacqueline Dubourg's parents for their daughter's hand."

"That's fine, Mama."

"We're in complete agreement about everything, aren't we, my son?"

"Yes, Mama."

"Do you have anything else to ask me ... anything else that you would like to discuss?"

"No, Mama."

■　■　■　■　■

That very evening, Maurice Floréal took Coralie to supper at "Aux Moujiks." The dinner was lively, the two table-companions extremely merry. Over champagne, Maurice announced to Coralie:

"My darling, this is a farewell dinner. I am devastated, but we are going to have to split up."

Coralie felt that she was going to throw up the homard flambé that she had just enjoyed.

"But, Maurice. Why?"

"For no good reason except that my mother thinks that a forty-year old man ought to be married, ought to start a family."

"And you agree with her?"

"And I fully agree with her."

"And that I am not 'marriageable'?"

Maurice hesitated for a moment. He suddenly took pity on this woman whose lips trembled against the fluted champagne glass from which she tried to swallow several mouthfuls. He put his hand on Coralie's and said softly:

"Darling, we have another conception of marriage and family than you. We don't have the same principles." And he added with a still softer voice, as if he were speaking to himself:

"No, Cora, you aren't 'marriageable' ... as my mother would say."

She got up suddenly and said to him, red-faced from humiliation:

"So, good-bye!"

"Wait, I'll take you home."

"No, that won't be necessary. I can walk as far as Ducoste Avenue. Don't bother with final gestures."

"Cora ... I ... We ... Wait."

"No, Maurice. Everything is finished here. Admit that you are relieved. Good-bye and good luck and ... thank you for everything."

And she dashed into the passage that led from the restaurant to Avenue des Dalles. Her heels twisted on the fine gravel. Angry tears flooded her face. She vaguely heard the cry of a man who called to her ....

"Coralie ... come back ... I love you ... Cora ...!"

Furious, she plunged into the night.

It was only after she got back to her room that she realized, when opening her handbag to take out the keys to her armoire, that Maurice Floréal had slipped a small envelope and a jewel-case inside. A splendid, solid gold chain, resembling a prisoner's chain, shone on the box's black velvet lining. The envelope contained a check for two thousand dollars and a card on which, under the name Maurice Floréal, Lawyer, were written two Latin words: "Tibi, semper."

Honestly, "to you, forever!" How ironic, this false "always" which ended so abruptly. And this supreme humiliation. Paid, paid handsomely like the deluxe prostitute she had become!

Tomorrow, without fail, she was going to return the chain and the check. Tomorrow, without fail. Her head throbbing with an atrocious migraine, her heart heavy, she finally fell into a restless sleep.

A night's sleep makes one wiser, and the next day, Coralie deposited the check in her bank account. After all, Maurice owed her at least some compensation. She had brought him sensual delight, three pleasure-filled years. That was well worth a little gift.

Now, she would have to readjust, spend prudently, learn how to restrain herself. While waiting, she felt disoriented. She missed the habits learned with Maurice Floréal. She was used to going out in the evening, to feeling a man's presence.

After several weeks, Coralie couldn't stand it any longer. There were plenty of taxis in the Champ de Mars area, and she had herself driven to the Ambiance Bar at Bicentenaire where she was sure to find some new faces to alleviate her solitude.

She got into the habit of choosing a table, always the same one, and of drinking several very strong cocktails while watching the dancers perform on the small, smoky dance floor. Sometimes a less timid dancer dared to invite this beautiful, high society woman appearing so unhappy, drinking her liquor straight, smoking a lot, and laughing too much when she was led in a deafening dance. Other times, she languished in the arms of a partner who held her tightly in position on the dance floor in a languid bolero. Soon she was known in all of the dance spots and nightclubs located under Bicentenaire's palm trees.

One evening, she went into the "Coq d'Argent" to have a drink and dance a little. She sat down at the bar and ordered a whisky with water from the bartender, whose face seemed vaguely familiar. She wasn't totally surprised when she heard her name called in a low voice:

"Madame … Madame Coralie …."

"You here, Marcel! You, a bartender?"

"Well yes, I'm no longer a private chauffeur, Madame. Besides, ever since I left your service, I haven't wanted to drive for anyone else. Thanks to a cousin, I became a bartender, as you can see. And during my free time, I drive a taxi on my own."

"But, it's been more than ten years, and you still remember me?"

"Can anyone ever forget you, Madame Cora? How could I forget you?"

In the eyes of the man, she saw fervent admiration. He looked her straight in the eye and said with a muted voice:

"I love you, Madame Cora. I have always loved you, but you were so far away, so distant, almost unreal."

He spoke well and had not lost his manners from having worked in dance spots and restaurants. On the contrary, his respectful boldness seemed stronger. He continued:

"May I offer you a drink, Madame Coralie?"

Amused by the zestiness of the adventure of being invited to have a drink by her former chauffeur, she agreed.

"With pleasure, Marcel. Come to my table over there."

"No, not here, Madame Coralie, but somewhere else. When I finish my work, if you want to."

Coralie measured for an instant the danger of the slippery slope on which she was sliding. Marcel was handsome, young, impetuous. Where might having a drink with her former chauffeur lead her? On the other hand, she was free, alone, without attachments, practically without relatives, not owing anything to anyone, not even herself.

She heard herself reply:

"Very well, Marcel. I'll wait for you."

At midnight, he took off his bartender's uniform, a kind of short vest with gold buttons on a black and red striped background. Then he disappeared several moments later. Quickly showered, freshly shaved, smelling of inexpensive lavender cologne, he had put on a white guayabera shirt over a pair of well-fitting gray trousers. His white shoes with black tips made him look like a Cuban dandy.

He took her by the arm and led her into the semi-darkness. You could not see two paces ahead of yourself, but he seemed to be used to the spot.

Coralie thought to herself:

"How many society women has he "picked up" in this way since he has been bartender at the "Coq d'Argent"?

She smiled to herself and said muttered under her breath:

"I'll stop it when I want to."

Marcel ordered some tasso de lambi, or conch, reputed to be an aphrodisiac, that she ate with the tips of her fingers, bursting out laughing each time the pepper made her cough. He taught her how to drink some coconut liqueur with gluttonous little gulps. Then they danced a bolero, a danzòn, a rumba. The jukebox played Pedro Cabral and Sonora Matancera without stopping.

She felt light, happy, beyond time, beyond life, beyond the sordid, monetary questions that would not fail to assault her soon. To forget, to forget all that for one moment, one evening, one night. After all, she was not yet forty, and life pulsated in her veins, in her stomach flattened against Marcel's, who held her now more tightly, cheek to cheek.

Suddenly, he became bolder. Half drunk, she moaned when he stuck his tongue in her left ear. She quivered with pleasure but pushed him away.

"Marcel, it's late, and I have to go home."

"I have my taxi over there. I'll take you home."

And the young man tightened his embrace, laying his warm hands on her curves and then crushing her against his aroused body.

Coralie groaned again:

"No ...."

But everything in her craved this young male. All of her being, deprived of love for weeks, yearned for Marcel's body. Without a word, he led her toward the blue Chevrolet parked on the other side of the boulevard. Still without talking, he opened the door for her, and she climbed into the spacious front seat, already defeated, consenting, willing. Marcel sped off towards La Mer Frappée. Suddenly, he stopped the car and literally tore Coralie from her seat, threw her in the back and, with one leap, was on top of her, searching in her skirts and brutally, without a word, without a caress, penetrated her, while Coralie's entire body, taut like a bow, met his aggressive snout-like organ.

They succeeded in having violent orgasms at the same time, and the loud, wild cry that Coralie uttered when she reached the summit of her pleasure vanished in the warm night. After several moments, they began again more calmly and together arrived at delightful enjoyment that spread itself into all of the limbs of a Coralie drowning in pleasure.

All along the return trip, they were silent. Marcel did not turn his face a single time towards Coralie who rested her buzzing head on the back of the cushion. What she had just felt was new, unique. Never during her adventurous life had she felt a similar incandescent jolt, a similar violent climax, a similar carnal union. Seated beside Marcel, she felt between her moist thighs something throbbing like another heart.

And she knew deep down that she was going to follow this man to the end of the cataclysm which had just toppled her into a world of flashing, red passion.

THE ELEVENTH STATION

DECEMBER 31: MUSSEAU

9:00 P.M.

"Damn, damn, damn, these wretched cufflinks refuse to stay put. Solanges! Solanges!"

Félix Nivel calls for assistance from his wife, Solanges, who emerges out of the bathroom with a green clay mask on her face. Her crow-black hair is rolled up in a forest of yellow and green rollers, transforming her head into an enormous pumpkin, overly ripe in some spots and much too green in others.

"Félix, why do you have to get dressed two hours before the party? I'm still not ready, and you're going to be all wrinkled before our guests arrive."

"And who is coming to the party this evening?"

"Let's see. The Rosenblums, two, the Alfred-Cruises, four .... The Leblancs aren't coming. They're having their own party. The Rainiers, three, the Pitous, two ...."

"Oh, those wimps. The woman particularly is such a simpleton!"

"But you told me yourself that they just purchased three hundred thousand dollars worth of materials from the Santeuil-Nivel Company, so ...."

"Yes, you're always right."

"And naturally, Marceau, your uncle and favorite, his wife, and their five daughters, seven ...

"Each one more stupid than the others. I wonder who will consent to marry those geese."

"Don't worry about it. They'll find husbands with their big dowries. One hundred thousand dollars each and a house in Juvénat Hills. With that, you don't stay an old maid, my love."

"So, how many people will there be at last count?"

"Let's add it all up." (And she counts painstakingly on her fingers several times over.) "They'll be eighteen of us. That's funny. I had planned for twenty-four place settings."

"You evidently didn't count us. You, me, Gratien-Félicien, his friend, Jerry, and Magali. That comes to exactly twenty-three. Who is the twenty-fourth guest?"

"Ah, I had forgotten Colonel Darcourt."

"Ah, the handsome colonel is invited, too?"

"We need to have friends from every social circle, and he has a lot of influence. He may be useful to us one of these days."

"He hovers around you most of all."

"Don't make me laugh. You'll make me crack my mask, and I'll give myself some horrid wrinkles. You know very well that I'm a faithful wife. It's not my fault if I'm attractive. It's that horrible magpie, Rose Leblanc, who spreads rumors about my having lovers. That old frump and her clan of old parakeets envy me."

Solanges is eager to cut this conversation short. As a matter of fact, she is the one gravitating around the handsome Colonel Darcourt. She literally harpooned him at the last reception at the Argentinean Embassy. He was finishing a dance with a beautiful American when she asked him point-blank to waltz with her. He accepted, and they have been playing a game of cat and mouse ever since. He is hooked now, and it is time to move on to serious things. Solanges Nivel's liaison with Hassim Hafez lasted more than ten years, and everyone, particularly her husband, knew about it. But the handsome Syrian was wealthy, opulent and an important customer of the Santeuil-Nivel Construction Materials Company. He built a chain of hotels in

Port-au-Prince, Port-Salut, and Labadie. People even said that the Nivels' daughter, Magali ....

Félix Nivel looks at himself in the large mirror that adorns their bedroom's immense closet. (Solanges went back into the bathroom and returned to her beauty care, designed that evening to make her dazzling in her guests' eyes and particularly in Darcourt's.) He looks at himself and sees himself as he is: ugly. He is a gnome, stout, short legged, and with an excessively long chest. His disproportionate arms make him look like an ape. He is putting on weight, and his bald head has an indentation in the middle. This irregularity in the surface makes his hair style all the more ludicrous. Bald, he lets a long strand of hair grow on the right side of his head. Every morning, after his shower, he sits down on a low stool in the bathroom, between Solanges' legs, and ever so carefully, lock by lock, she recovers his skull with this pseudo-fringe that she plasters down with hair oil.

He recognizes his ugliness, and that is why he closes his eyes to his wife's escapades. People have even spread the rumor that his daughter, his cherished Magali, is actually Hafez's child. That is not true. That must be false. He loves this child too much. Somewhere in his body something would cry out if this child was not his. She is the being in the world he loves the most, and he would die if his daughter, Magali ... But after all, her grandfather, Félicien, was a very good-looking man and Coralie, his mother, a beauty. He inherited this considerable ugliness from his father, Gratien, but he does not have his kind-heartedness.

If he keeps Solanges, it is because she is beautiful, a superb, fleshy, dark-haired woman. When he married her she was poor, very poor, and very attractive, and she exchanged herself for wealth. She has served him mightily by her tact and her sense of beneficial connections. Basically, she does not owe Felix anything. She has fulfilled her contract and paid her quota.

Just the same, she is a head taller than he is, and when they are somewhere together, Félix remains far from his wife and seeks the company of other women, small, squat, and scorned like him.

Besides, if he has kept Solanges in spite of her adventures, it is because she is remarkable in public relations. An excellent hostess, she knows whom to invite and when to invite, and more than one dinner invitation from his wife has brought him some big contracts.

His son, Gratien Félicien, just as ugly as his father but more congenial, is studying management at MIT in Boston. He came back home for vacation with an American friend, a little homosexual around the edges, but young people go through phases, and so much the better if they go through them somewhere else, far from the eyes and the gossip of Port-au-Prince's backyards. By the time he comes back here, we'll get him back on track.

Colonel Darcourt is the only one who annoys him. Almost six feet tall, the colonel overshadows him still more. With a slender build, broad chest, and square shoulders, he is a superb human specimen. People sense that he is manly without being brutal, pleasant without being obsequious. His rugged face is lit up by a brilliant smile revealing a dazzling set of teeth. Each time Colonel Darcourt smiles, Nivel frowns, pinching his lips together over his yellowed, crooked stumps. What annoys him still more is that Solanges, this time around, seems to be completely crazy about him. It is no longer a fashionable, passing fancy between two dinners or two bridge or canasta games. He knows his wife, and he feels that she is caught on the handsome soldier's epaulettes. If she is not already his mistress, she is bound to be before very long.

And he has to welcome this fop, this swashbuckler, to his table. Only an unforeseen event of major proportions can stop Darcourt from sleeping with Solanges, perhaps this evening or tomorrow.

He rages inwardly and is in a very bad mood. If Darcourt at least had another liaison, or if he were thinking about having a wife. But the seductive colonel is still single. *Nèg sa a derefize marye; li pran madanm nèg ki enterese li.* This guy refuses to get married. He goes off with whatever married women he is interested in.

"Damn, damn, damn," rages Félix Nivel. His evening is ruined in advance. Besides, all of these idle, lazy people are going to come to feast at his expense. He is furious.

And it is at this moment that the house boy comes to announce to him that there is a lady asking for him ... she says she is Coralie Santeuil.

"*Tonmat vèt* ... What a nuisance ... Damn, damn, damn! That is all I needed."

"*Fout li deyò. Fout li deyò, mete chen dèyèl.* Kick her out. Kick her out. Set the dogs on her. I don't want to see her. Don't let her stay. Make her go away right now without wasting any time," he blurts out.

What would his guests say if they knew that the mother of the powerful Gratien-Félix Nivel, the extremely rich potentate, is a former brothel prostitute turned public beggar to boot?

He foams, he thunders, he shouts. He holds it against his mother who has ruined all of his opportunities, who humiliates him by her very existence. He holds it against her for having made him so ugly.

"*Sak fè li pa mouri?* Why doesn't she just die?"

And Magali appears. The gentle presence of the innocent little girl calms him down like a cold shower.

"What's the matter, Papa? Why have you lost your temper? Why are you shouting so loud?"

"It's nothing. Well, it is something. The boy came to disturb me on behalf of some kind of a beggar woman, a poor woman who comes all the way here to Musseau to pester me by asking for money. On New Year's Eve! I have the right to relax in my own home at the end of a day's work, at the end of a particularly difficult year. *Jouk isit la!* She appears, even here!"

Magali runs a calming hand across her father's forehead.

"Don't bother, Papa. I'll take care of her. Don't worry. Calm down. Angry outbursts are bad for your blood pressure. Come on ... smile ... That's it!"

Félix Nivel forces a smile. Fortunately, Magali does not know who this unwelcome beggar is.

He is not taking into account the servants who always know the deepest, darkest secrets of the best families. A long time ago, their whispers and their hints informed the young girl, and she knows, yes, she knows who she is, this visitor her father disowns, spurns, and chases away with such a racket.

She goes down to the pantry which is brimming with various delicacies. She prepares a plate full of turkey, ham, salad, mushroom-flavored rice, and a large cup of bouillon, and she hurries with the tray toward the awkward, wobbling silhouette moving off slowly at the end of the path decorated with garlands of electric lanterns and multicolored balloons.

She almost runs toward Coralie who turns around.

"Madame, please, come and rest here in this little gazebo. Here you are. Sit there in that lounge-chair and eat. Go ahead."

And Magali looks at Coralie who, having swallowed all of her pride, eats the sumptuous meal eagerly.

"The poor woman is at the end of her rope," thinks the gentle adolescent.

"Take your time."

"But I'm disturbing you and perhaps delaying you. Your parents ...."

" ... aren't concerned about me at this hour. I'm all ready, and I comb my hair so quickly. I prefer keeping you company. Go on. Drink some more of this bouillon. It isn't too hot."

"Thank you, my child, thank you. You are good. God will bless you," sighs Coralie.

"And now, rest. Take a nice, little nap. Go ahead. Close your eyes … There … That's it."

And Magali places a light kiss on Coralie's forehead. Beneath the unexpected caress, Coralie's eyes close, while two large tears roll down her ravaged face. The child murmurs softly as if she does not want to be heard by the poor woman who now seems to be sleeping.

"Rest … grandmother …."

Then feeling relieved, she goes back to the villa where, on the illuminated front steps, Solanges and Félix Nivel in evening dress, welcome their first guests.

TWELVE

For three months, Coralie was no more than a female in heat who had met her ideal mate. Every evening, she went down by taxi to the Vert Luron where she waited submissively for Marcel until midnight. Then, from midnight until dawn, she gave herself to him, enjoying their embraces several times during the night. She did not go back to her place until the wee hours of the morning, her body still quivering with pleasure, and thinking only about seeing once again the lover to whom she was sensuously bound.

During the day, after her late arousal, she remained stretched out on her bed, motionless, weak, asking herself a thousand questions. What would happen to her if Marcel, who had undoubtedly known so many similar adventures, left her? What would happen to her if Madame Santeuil, Marceau, and her son learned about the depraved life that she was leading with a former servant?

She trembled, cried, and smoked a lot. Already very thin, she lost still more weight, as if she were burned up with desire and consumed with passion. She swore that she was going to leave Marcel and never return to the Vert Luron. She swore to stop and pull herself together.

But the fire in her body did not go out. She had to have this man every night, immediately, now.

And at eight o'clock in the evening, she got up, feverish, and dressed simply in order to be stripped of her clothing more quickly. She had abandoned gloves, costly jewels, excessively high heels. She was no more than a tall woman, completely ordinary, who waited with breathless anxiety the one who had disclosed sexual pleasures, sensual delights to her.

Marcel's impassioned embraces left her entirely happy, blissful, deeply soothed, and she lived for the moments when she forgot everything in his arms, becoming herself an ardent lover, a docile partner, and a passionate reveler at the same time.

For three or four months, Coralie lived this regime of alternation between mad passion and long periods of despondency. During this time, all she did each day was to wait to rejoin the man who subjugated her as if she were attached to him by an invisible thread. Completely wrapped up in this intense sexual life she was discovering, she no longer noticed anything around her, not even the disapproving look of Madame Saint-René, the woman in charge of the boarding house, who up until the present had shown a lot of consideration and respect for her. The servants' sneers, allusions, and outbursts of laughter early in the morning when they ran into Coralie, exhausted, wild-looking from heightened sexual activities, were oblivious to the young woman who was completely engrossed in her private hurricane.

She was so involved that she did not notice right away that she had not had her period for two months. She had lost all sense of time, and it is with terror that she looked at the wall calendar where she used to jot down her meetings with Floréal, an appointment with dressmaker, hairdresser, or manicurist.

Abashed, she waited for night and, as usual, took a taxi which dropped her off at the Vert Luron without her having to give that address to the driver. This particular one had already driven her several times to the restaurant-bar-dance hall, and when she got out of the vehicle and handed him a green bill, he looked at her with a mischievous wink and a chuckle which seemed to say:

"Soon, little lady, it will be my turn."

A violent nausea overcame her, and she stopped behind the oleander hedge bordering the path to vomit for a long time. She felt relieved and went to sit down at a small table in the back as usual. Ages ago, Marcel had abandoned the tone of deferential politeness that had marked the distance that once existed bewtween them. In public, he treated her as if they were living together and now took pleasure in showing her off. Just think about it. A beautiful mulatto from the haute, gwo moun, gwo chabrak, a big shot, and who was the mistress of Marcel Sibert, taxi driver, bartender, and macho!

He noticed right away that she was different. Her eyes did not have that fire promising burning caresses. She was lifeless, disheveled, with circles under the eyes, her mouth trembling.

"What's wrong with you? What's the matter, Cora?"

"Marcel, I am … I am … well … I am pregnant."

The man opened his eyes wide and swallowed several times in succession.

"Ou vle dim ou ansent? *You're telling me you're pregnant?"*

With one breath, Cora answered, her mouth dry:

"Yes, for two months."

"So what are you going to do?"

"Kòman sa mwen pral fè? *What do you mean, what am I going to do?"*

Coralie too abandoned the borrowed language, this French which too often is more of a barrier than a communication between Haitians.

"Kòman sa mwen pral fè? *What do you mean, what am I going to do?" she repeated.* Ou vle di sa nou pral fe? *Aren't you going to tell me what we are going to do, Marcel?* Fòk ou marye avèm vit pou bay pitit la yon non. *You had better marry me quickly so the child will have a name."*

Marcel looked at her, then suddenly let out an enormous burst of laughter that ended up disappearing under the thatched roof.

"Moun pa marye ak de fanm non, Cora. *You can't be married to two women, Cora.*"

" ...?"

"Madan marye-m Nouyòk depi dezan. Tout papyem nan ambasad. *My wife has been in New York for two years. All of my papers are at the embassy.* Konsil la banm randevou, m san lè pati. *I have an appointment with the consulate. Any day now, I can leave the country.*"

And since Coralie did not seem to understand, he added:

"Map vole, Cora, map kite Ayiti tout bon. *I'm going to take off, Cora. I'm leaving Haiti for good. I'm not doing anything serious here. I'll be working in New York for a lot of money, and soon after that, I'll send for my old mother and my two children who are with her in Petit-Goâve.*"

Stunned, Cora heard herself ask:

"Ou gen pitit deja? Ou gen lòt pitit? *You already have children? You have other children?*"

Naively, she had thought that Marcel Sibert, the Nivel's ex-chauffeur, would have been happy and proud to know that she, Coralie Santeuil, was expecting his child, that he would jump at the opportunity to marry her and to regularize their situation all the while climbing up several rungs on the social ladder. Instead of that, here he was, the idiot, completely stupid, completely oblivious to the special favor that she had granted him by allowing him to inseminate the womb of an important society woman.

"So, what am I going to do?"

"M pa konnen non Ti Manman. *I don't know, woman.* Degaje ou. *Do whatever you want.*"

"I have to find a solution. How?"

"Degaje ou jete pitit la. Try to get rid of the baby. That's all I can say to you, because mwen pa ladan, I'm staying out of it. Ou tande mwen. Mwen kraze yon kite sa. Male. M vole! You hear me. I want nothing to do with this. I'm out of here. I'm gone!"

Violently pushing his chair away, he made it fall, and the noise struck Cora's ears like a hellish racket. With a mocking smile at the corner of his fleshy lips, Marcel bent over her in his role as a zealous, obsequious chauffeur.

"My regards, Madame Nivel, my very deepest regards!"

Coralie slipped off her chair in a faint.

▪ ▪ ▪ ▪ ▪

Who brought her back to the boarding house "La Belle Quarteronne"? She never knew. She found herself in her bed with the two servants, Marta and Clara, who were nudging one another, looking at her mischieviously. Of course, they saw that Madame Cora was "a byen fè." People from Les Cayes don't say "pregnant" or "with child." Those are bad words. Instead, they say you're doing well, because they respect you even though what you have done may not be proper.

Overcome with encephalitis, Coralie was very close to death. In case of an accident she had asked Madame Saint-René to contact Rose Darcey Leblanc, who lived in Bourdon and Lise Alphonsin, who had her clinic in Chemin des Dalles. Both came faithfully to their friend's bedside. Rose Leblanc, thanks to her marriage to Hervé Leblanc, a wealthy industrialist, was not very busy caring for her own home, so she spent her days at delirious Coralie's bedside. She bathed her temples and gave her the medications that Lise, for her part, prescribed and purchased on a regular basis.

The two of them saved Coralie's life, but when she confided in Lise about her scarcely visible condition due to her extreme thinness, the doctor was strict; she was approaching her fifth month, and it was no longer possible to interrupt her pregnancy. In spite of the mother's illness, the child was robust, healthy, and only asking to live.

"An abortion in your state of health and at this stage of your pregnancy would be fatal."

"But I don't want to have this child!"

"Nonsense! The Santeuils took Félix away from you. Heaven is sending you a child to fill the void in your life, a support in your old age. You'll see. This child will be your reason for living. See how strong it already is and how it's kicking you."

"But my illness must have taken its toll on the child. Is it possible that it be deformed? handicapped?"

"Not at all, my dear. Pitit sa a vin pou l viv, kite l viv! This baby wants to live. Let the baby live!"

Four months later, hospitalized thanks to Lise Alphonsin, Coralie gave birth to a second son who was named Robert and was the godson of Lise, who took charge of everything. But when it came time for Coralie to return to the boarding house "La Belle Quarteronne," Madame Saint-René flatly refused.

"Madame Nivel, I was just about to ask you to leave my boarding house because your excesses made the help and the other boarders gossip. All of us were aware of your conduct, and the rumor about your pregnancy spread like a house on fire throughout the entire neighborhood."

"But this is a boarding house. It's like a hotel. I think I'm free to come and go as I please. As far as I know, I'm not accountable to anyone."

"It is possible that you think like that, Madame Nivel, but my boarding house is not a fly-by-night hotel."

Coralie's entire face reddened. So, the darati, the crabby oldlady, had noticed that Marcel sometimes slept in Coralie's bedroom up there and vanished only at dawn. She now evaluated her imprudence; she had no place to go.

"Madame Saint-René.."

"Madame Nivel, it is useless to insist. I was just about to ask you for the room, but you fell so seriously ill that, as a good Christian, I waited for your convalescence and the birth of your child before asking you to empty out your space. The time has come."

Coralie tried to show her Robert, who was sleeping like an angel in her arms:

"Madame …."

"It's no use, Madame. Besides, your room is already rented to someone else, and I had all of your things packed up. You'll find your boxes and cases under the porch. There is nothing missing. You can be assured of that. I supervised everything myself. Good-bye, Madame Nivel, and good luck."

And the tidy old lady with her Spanish chignon turned her back without waiting any longer in the event that Coralie, crushed, might come up with some kind of retort.

She was forced to take a taxi to Bois Verna, where Lise Alphonsin had bought an old gingerbread house she was lovingly restoring. Without a husband or child, Doctor Lise Alphonsin lived alone with Charlesia, her old servant, and was passionately fond of four things: reading, playing the piano, gardening, and naturally healing children. A well-known pediatrician, she brought a heart of gold to the practice of this profession which demanded as much dedication as knowledge. This woman alone had boundless love, and she welcomed with open arms Cora and the baby, this godson who satisfied an unfulfilled desire for motherhood in her.

Robert was going to grow up at the side of this exceptional woman and be educated with all of the passion that Lise held in reserve after the destruction of her own love life. Charlesia waited hand and foot on Coralie and her son. Her natural casualness and easy-going character quickly soothed Coralie's sorrows.

Just at the time she was recovering from the jolts of her unstable life, Aline contacted her directly by phone. How did Madame Santeuil know where to find her? She had only given her new address to Auguste Percier and to the young clerks in Floréal's office. Having lived so long abroad, the poor woman did not understand anything about the Haitian grapevine. She did not know that Aline had not given up following her every step and that her stepmother knew everything about her "misconduct." The phone call was intended to tell her some bad news. What good could ever come to her from Aline Santeuil?

"Coralie, it's you?"

"Yes, Aline, what's the matter?"

"Your father died yesterday evening at nine o'clock. The funeral is Thursday afternoon at four o'clock at Pax Villa."

A click. That's it, It's over.

Exit Félicien. Coralie is surprised not to shed one tear for this father she loved so much, but whose weak character turned her over to a nasty, greedy stepmother. From Félicien she gets her passive character, this tendency to submit to any will stronger than her own and to let herself be overwhelmed by adversity. That is the only legacy he has left her.

Legacy ... legacy! And suddenly Coralie remembers the paper that Aline had wrung from her twelve years ago at Félix's baptism. She gave up in advance her part of the inheritance from Félicien Santeuil's estate. And now, she depends solely on the Santeuils' good will for her own and little Robert's survival. Just the same, her son is also Félicien's grandchild. He has a right to something. Surely Aline will not change her mind about her stratagem, but Marceau ... Marceau whose business has grown fivefold thanks to the capital acquired from Coralie and Félix. Maybe Marceau will agree to give her back a part of her inheritance from their father for Robert.

And Coralie rushes to the little boy's cradle, takes the baby, and kisses him briskly. The mother's hug is so strong, so crushing, that the frightened child begins to cry.

And while Charlesia comes trotting along on her old legs, Coralie suddenly bursts into hysterical tears.

THE TWELFTH STATION

DECEMBER 31: MORNE HERCULE

MIDNIGHT

How long did Coralie, the reprobate, sleep in the garden house at Felix's? Did she dream that her son's daughter called her "Grandmother?" A great sweetness flooded her soul. She feels totally bathed in an interior light and somehow redeemed by that kiss and that name, "Grandmother." She forgot her meandering search, the slow, painful walk which forced her on the road looking for life-saving money. Something resembling hope quivers in a corner of her ravaged soul. She has approached Pétion-Ville, gone around the market zone, and now limps towards Morne Hercule. They told her it was number one hundred and ten on the right. That is where the young director of the Bank for Reconstruction and Investment lives. Already a bank director and so efficient and brilliant! He has only one fault: he is a womanizer with a fondness for beautiful, visiting foreigners searching for exciting adventures with handsome, well-established Haitian partners. He prefers that over the complications of an intrigue with a young society girl. With those foolish young ladies, it is immediately question of proposals, appearances, engagements rings, mothers-in-law, dowries … Ugh! What a breed! It is much more practical to have a liaison with a beautiful tourist just passing through. One time, two times, and then, hey presto! On to the next!

This evening he is expecting Hélène Beauchamp, a Canadian tourist recommended to him by a friend at the bank. Morally lax, this woman offers herself to all of the handsome Haitians who court her. Court her is really an exaggeration. Do you want her? There she is. And afterwards, good-bye, good night. On to the next of these gentlemen. Whose turn is it? This beautiful Hélène doesn't lack admirers, and the intimate New Year's Eve dinner the "Namki" caterer prepared for Robert is already on the table.

Soft, subdued light, silver candelabras dripping with perfumed candles, a floor-length embroidered linen cloth on a table installed in the bedroom where the bed with its freshly laundered sheets invites loving revels.

In order to be free to lead this life of a bachelor on the prowl, Robert left the home of his adoptive mother, Lise Alphonsin. He adores and worships her. But in the end, at her house, everything is too orderly, too aristocratic, really too stuffy. Even ridiculous! A bit too traditional Haitian, making him feel uncomfortable. In Mama Lise's house, imagine an orgy with a fast, young Canadian woman met by chance. Impossible!

Robert laughs to himself at his joke. In truth, what he loves is love. He falls in love with every pretty woman he meets, and each new conquest banishes the previous one. He knows very well that some day he will have to settle down, set goals, marry a naive young thing or a rich girl or perhaps even the two combined. But for the time being, he is completely involved in his adventure with Hélène, the pretty, free-spirited woman from the far north.

Energized, he gave himself a fresh shave, sprinkled himself with Viking Noir perfume, and slipped on white flannel trousers and a cotton knit polo shirt which shows off his tennis muscles. He is pleased about the evening celebration and relishes in advance the pleasures awaiting him. Everything is ready to welcome his New Year's Eve guest: foie gras, lobster, caviar, Caesar salad, exquisite wine, and champagne. The calm, silent waiter sent by the caterer is finishing setting the table on which several Regency roses in a Daum vase are looking elegant.

Robert quivers with impatience and desire.

Hélène can't be much longer; she will arrive any time now. That is she. The doorbell pierces the air saturated with heady perfumes. Robert rushes to the front door even before the house boy; he opens it and finds himself face to face with Coralie. His mother! What a letdown!

"You, Mama, at this hour ... but ... but ... it is almost midnight. Mama, where are you coming from?"

And Cora tells her son about her long search across the city, her urgent need for rent money. She tells him everything, everything. Her long day, fruitless visits, Félix's welcome, Magali's gentleness ....

Moved, Robert takes her hands, those poor hands that have suffered so much. He kisses them and berates himself, with his carefree life as a handsome ladies man and successful businessman, for having forgotten this mother, this true mother, who loved him enough to entrust him to another woman better able to raise him.

"Mama, I don't want you to be lacking anything anymore. Each month, you'll come to Mama Lise's house to get a small sum, and I am going to rent you a house at Pétion-Ville, at La Boule, in town, wherever you want. You'll see, you'll see. I'm going to make you forget everything. Mama, oh, Mama."

The mother and son stay clasped in one another's arms, interrupting one another and talking at the same time. Robert has forgotten Hélène. Coralie tells him about the last part of her wretched life. He reproaches her for not having said anything to him about it, and he reproaches himself as well for not having tried to find out.

At about one o'clock in the morning, Robert leads his long-lost mother toward the cold supper in front of the wide eyes of the disapproving waiter. What! Mr. Robert did all of this preparation for this *granmoun*, this old lady, this *epav*, this derelict, this beggar? *Gen moun ki pa byen nan tèt wi*! *Li do fou*! Some people are really crazy! He must be out of his mind!

Hélène did not come, and Robert does not give a damn. Tomorrow, he will learn that she preferred taking a midnight swim at Chalet sur Mer with another lover. What does it matter? One lost, ten found. That kind of woman is not very fussy about the adventures she came to look for in Haiti.

While waiting, mother and son chatter freely. The fine food and champagne go to Coralie's head, restoring the former sparkle to her eyes and causing the formation on her lips of the crystal-clear laugh belonging to the beautiful, seductive, irresistible Coralie Santeuil.

"Wait, Mama, I must give you your rent money. I would have given you even more, but all I have in cash in the house is this hundred dollar bill I'm giving you. You know, I only use credit cards or my checkbook. So, from January third on, I'll deposit for you whatever amount you need. And then, we'll go together to look for a little house. Mama, Mama, I love you very much, and I'm happy. Come along, I'll take you back in my car."

And they proceed to leave when the strident, insistent doorbell rings.

It is Hélène. She is late because she stopped to have a drink with some compatriots who detained her. She apologizes to Robert, who, ill at ease, introduces her to Coralie. He is suddenly very embarrassed to say "my mother" and finally decides to say:

"Madame Santeuil, one of my mother's friends."

And quite ashamed, he murmurs in Coralie's ear:

"Forgive me for not taking you home, Mama. Try to find a taxi. Happy Hew Year, and I'll see you soon."

Leading the woman who is already chuckling about her anticipated pleasure, Robert disappears inside the bedroom.

Finding a taxi at this hour, a January first at dawn, with a single five hundred gourde bill! It is true that Robert may have thought she had other smaller amounts somewhere on her, in her bra, for instance. That is the place where women without handbags tuck their money.

What does it matter if she starts out on the road again, alone and numb with cold in her thin, threadbare dress. Her heart feels warm. She has rediscovered an affection, her son's, perhaps two, with young Magali's tenderness. She is no longer all alone. She does not really care if Robert keeps his promises or not. What counts is that he loves her. He loves her, oh miracle of Saint Sylvester!

She is going to start out again calmly, slowly. She moves shakily from Morne Hercule to the exit of Pétion-Ville's cemetery. Then she begins the Delmas road. She smiles thinking about Robert, the womanizer, who, up there in his isolated villa, has undressed the young foreigner.

THIRTEEN

Aline had announced Coralie's father's funeral to her just as she would have to anyone outside the family. *Félicien's eldest daughter was not summoned to the two o'clock afternoon wake in order to receive, along with Aline and Marceau, the condolences offered by friends, acquaintances, clients, and employees of the Santeuils.*

"I won't let them walk all over me this time. I'll be at the funeral home at two o'clock, and I'll force all of those hypocrites to shake my hand just like Aline's and Marceau's," Coralie says to Lise.

She dressed as simply as she could in a gray linen suit and a white sun hat with a black ribbon. Black stockings, shoes, handbag and gloves completed her very dignified, very elegant outfit. She admired herself in the large mirror in her bedroom. The birth of her second child had heightened her beauty. She had filled out without gaining weight. She no longer appeared distraught or to be burning up inside as she had during her affair with Marcel Sibert. In spite of several wrinkles on her forehead and the suggestion of some fine lines next to her temples, Coralie Santeuil remained a very beautiful woman favored, rather than burdened, by her forty years.

Not being particularly large, the family, that is to say, Aline and Félix on one side, Marceau, his sickly wife, and his daughters on the other, framed the casket of a Félicien dead in his nineties, and who was so shriveled up that he seemed to have been placed in a coffin that was too big for him.

Flowers, dozens of wreaths in all possible shapes and colors with their blue, purple, violet, pink or orange ribbons, created a brightly colored garland around the room which gave testimony to the Santeuil family's social position. Well, it is not to the poor dead that people give wreaths and sheaves of flowers at funerals. They could not care less. It is to those who stay behind, to the living, especially if they are very rich, that these superb floral arrangements are given. It is a way of saying to acquaintances, "See, we are your friends. Do not forget us at your parties and in your business ventures."

Coralie, who had only a vague idea of the financial power that the Santeuils had acquired, was surprised that her father, so old, ill for so long, and withdrawn from the world, would have kept so many friendships alive. Resolutely and without greeting anybody, after having lodged a quick kiss on the head of her son who was too surprised to react, she sat down on Aline's side in the chair next to him.

And then followed the processions of visitors who were not truly sad, hands that one shakes, the

"Thank you. Thank you."

"You have all of my sympathy."

"Condolences."

"We share your sorrow."

"Have courage. Have courage."

"It is a blessing for him."

"He is no longer suffering."

"He is better off where he is now."

"God help you."

"It is a blessing for you."

"He is protecting you from up above".

More than once, Coralie was overcome with laughter seeing people, who would have ignored her had they met her in the street, obligated to greet her cordially and shake her hand energetically, or give her a friendly kiss as if they were friends who suddenly recognized her.

"Oh! Cora, what a joy to see you again!"

"Dear Coralie, when did you come back from your travels?"

Deep down inside, she was amused by all of this and forgot to watch Aline stiffening up even more and pinching her lips until they were practically invisible. She felt her stepmother completely wrapped up in suppressed anger and was delighted at the trick she had just played on her.

When it came time to remove the body, Coralie followed Aline and Félix to place a last conventional kiss on her father's cold forehead because she no longer felt anything for the remains that were there, for the old, unknown man, this old, shrunken, dried-up stem.

While the employees closed the casket and removed the wreathes, Aline approached Cora and with a dark look hissed between her teeth:

"You will pay me for this, Cora, and it will cost you plenty."

Coralie shuddered. Since her oppressed childhood, she had known that this woman never made empty threats. She did not dare go to the cemetery to deal once again with all of the flatterers who would consider it a duty to go to see the burial of Félicien, whom they were as unconcerned about as the plague. It was beyond her strength. Over the tomb, Aline could, much better than in the parlor, hold her in her piercing look, and she was afraid of bravely facing again that relentless woman on whom she depended for her livelihood.

Three days after her father's funeral, Coralie received a registered document. It was a summons to appear in court about a matter pertaining to her. Panic stricken, she asked Lise to find her a resourceful lawyer, not too "costly," who would agree to defend her for reasonable fees. Lise obtained the services of an honest, experienced lawyer, but he had few oratorical skills, and did not hold his own against the arguments drawn up by the Santeuils' counsel.

Aline spared Coralie nothing. Everything was brought out into the open: her stubborn, insubordinate temperament; her bad tendencies visible from the time she started school causing her dismissal from the boarding school for having attempted to corrupt her companions; her marriage for money to a wealthy man who wanted to save her from herself and who, in return, she had shamelessly deceived; her extra-marital affairs; then finally, her total abandonment of her child for eight, long years during which time she had openly led a life of debauchery and scandal; her affair with a German officer which got her into trouble with the French government after the Liberation; her return to Haiti where, in spite of the generous offer of Madame Aline Santeuil to return home to live with her family at her son's side, she had preferred to live in a hotel in order to give free reign to her nymphomania; her notorious affair with a young lawyer from the capital who, tired of her insatiable appetite for debauchery, had left her to marry a respectable person; her thirst for pleasure that had led her to frequent alone all of the places of debauchery in the capital in search of fleeting adventures, and finally, her love affair with a former servant with whom she had had a child conceived in adultery because the man was married.

For all of these reasons, the minor's guardian, Gratien Félix Nivel, and the family council requested that Madame Coralie Santeuil-Nivel be stripped in perpetuity of her maternal rights, that she be strictly forbidden to frequent or even try to approach her son, and that the fiscal custody of the child be entrusted to her maternal uncle, Louis-Marceau Santeuil.

And the Santeuils' lawyer concluded:

"May it please your Honor to remove the young, innocent boy from the influence of a mother who does not have the moral qualities needed to raise a child and who could only, through her contact, lead him along the scabrous paths of vice and depravation."

Coralie was destroyed, especially since none of the facts held against her were debatable. Everything was true, even if distorted, and how could she explain that life had jostled and mistreated her; that weak and without any preparation, she had only the means nature had given her to defend herself: her beauty, her charm.

Aline avenged herself cruelly. Once more, Coralie was crushed by the vindictiveness of this woman who, after having ruined her materially, struck the final blow by demolishing her morally and socially.

Strengthened by their rights, irreproachable principles, and powerful fortune, the Santeuils destroyed Coralie once and for all and flung her back again into the life of perdition that she would like to have been able to give up.

The following month, no check arrived from Floréal's office. All she had was the meager resource from the small sum, always unpredictable besides, that Auguste Percier paid her. Certain months, in December for example, it was one hundred dollars, sometimes, eighty, other times, sixty. The preceding month, she had received only forty dollars. How can one live on that when one is not working, when one does not know how to find employment?

Too weak and too tired to fight, Coralie plunged into a world reeking of tobacco and alcohol. She started crawling the bars again in the evening and began to give herself to unknown men for a few dollars in order to at least cover the cost of little Robert's food. She was no longer thinking about herself, but about providing for the support of the only child remaining to her, the only son she would ever have loved.

How was Doctor Lise Alphonsin, so proper and so strict about her behavior, going to tolerate that Coralie, living in her home, continued to lead a loose life? Very quickly the reproaches, the implications poisoned their relationship. And one day, out of the blue, Lise proposed to a more scattered than usual Coralie:

"And if I were to adopt Robert?"

"Adopt Robert?"

"Yes legally. Properly. I'll give him my name, and he'll become my heir. What can you do for him? You don't have any skills; you cannot work nor do you know how to work; you don't have any sense of discipline in your life. My poor Coralie, we must be realistic. You do

not have what it takes to raise a child. Robert is my godson, almost my son already.

"But I want to keep my child."

"You want to keep him only for yourself because basically you are profoundly egotistical. You want to keep him to play with him sometimes, tickle him, read him stories in the evening when, by chance, you are here at his bedtime. You love him for yourself, like a trinket, like an entertaining toy. How will you bring him up? Where will you live with him? Undoubtedly, in one of your bars? You must only think about Robert and do what is best for this child."

"But I want to give him the best ...."

"How, Coralie? How? You had only your beauty and a certain kind of touching naiveté that made others want to help you. But look at yourself. You have gotten old, and the night life is wearing you down every day, or rather every night, even more. Banm pitit la Cora; banm mwen li, lap pi bon ni pou ou, ni pou li. Give me the child, Cora; give him to me. It would be good for you and for him."

For months, Lise made the same request and Coralie, disconcerted, finally realized that her friend was right. Yes, for Robert, it would be better if Lise adopted him. Cora needed to forget herself and think more about the well-being of the little boy who was soon going to celebrate his second birthday and who knew Charlesia, whom he called Chasa, and Lise, his mama Yise, better than his true mother, always away when he was awake and always asleep when she was at home.

The papers signed by Coralie without opposition made the little fellow officially Robert Alphonsin, and the next day, Lise let Coralie know that she had to leave her house.

"You understand, Cora. The child must not in any way be subjected to your influence and become attached to you. I alone must bring him up. Later, I'll explain to him who you are, who he is, and how he became my son. I promise you truly that he will know that you are his mother."

"But what is going to become of me, and where am I going to go?"

"Cora, it is time for you to take charge of your life. Try to find some work, just anything. Take your destiny into your own hands. It is time for you to stand up, to face life blow by blow. Grapple with it. In short, fight back."

"Lise, Lise, at least let me come to sleep in your home. I will scarcely see Robert, I promise. Lise, don't chase me out."

"No, what you will see of Robert and what he will see of you would still be too much for the moral education that I want to give him. Get back on your feet, Cora, and then you'll become worthy of my friendship and Robert's admiration, if not of his love."

"But working. That's easier said than done. Doing what and where?"

"Charlesia has a nephew who is a foreman in a baseball factory. She can speak to him on your behalf. You'll begin at the bottom of the ladder, but with your intelligence, you'll make yourself appreciated, and you'll advance. At least you know how to hold a needle!"

"Of course. Are you forgetting the beautiful, embroidered work we did in boarding school? I was even better at embroidery than you and Rose."

"Perfect. These baseballs are sewn by hand, and Haitian workers are known for the quality of their workmanship. You'll see. You'll get along just fine, and you'll at least be able to earn a decent living. Good luck, Cora. Cheer up!"

The following Monday, Coralie was hired at the Haitian American Softball Company. At the beginning, it was very difficult for her because the material to sew on was real leather. And even though the holes through which the needle passed were perforated in advance by the machine, the effort needed was considerable, especially because the stitching had to be done under the surface rather than above it.

Coralie slaved and soon became highly skilled. So as not to be far from work, she rented herself a small room at Martissant in the home of a friendly, hard-working woman who had a shop and who took in one renter, by necessity a woman, to occupy the room belonging to her daughter who had left to study in Canada. The woman shared her morning and evening meals with Coralie in return for a slight supplement. At noon, she lunched with the other working women on fritailles, *fried meat and plantains,* marinades, *fried dumplings, and* patés cordés, *fried, stuffed twists, sold in the factory's grill.*

She identified herself with this humble milieu, shared the concerns, listened to the problems about missing or non-existent husbands, sick children, about mò yo voye sou matant mwen, *the spirit of death they sent to an aunt, about* lougawou kap manje timoun, *the boogy man who eats children,* or the matlòt ki vin kale madan marye, *the mistress who comes to beat the wife … and she was surprised to have lived for so long unacquainted with this crowded, shimmering, colorful life that teemed around her.*

Coralie tried courageously to fit into the existence made up of daily heroism, content to have as her only distractions reading used magazines bought in a second-hand store and watching television in the evening with the good Madame Arsène, her landlady, good, old B Westerns in which Allan Ladd and Ronald Reagan triumphed. Her body, as if asleep, dead tired from a healthy fatigue, did not torment her anymore and she wondered what had happened to the Coralie who, to quench the big, red flame that arose from her womb, prowled the streets of Port-a-Prince at night in search of a Marcel Sibert.

Sunday mornings, she was present at a strange, bucolic ceremony that made her happy. Madame Arsène had a milk cow brought into the courtyard from the nearby countryside. This task had fallen to Sylvanne, Madame Arsène's little niece, who invariably balked:

"Matant mwen pè bèf la wi. *Auntie, I'm afraid of the cow.*"

"Hany! Annavan, tire bèt la ban mwen. *Hey! Come on, milk the cow for me.*"

"Matant lap banm kout pye wi. *Auntie, it's kicking me."*

"Mare janm li. *Tie up its legs."*

And crouching behind the beast, Sylvanne approached, armed with a rope she used to tie together the animal's hind legs. Then, she slipped a big enamel pail under the pink, silky, rounded udders of the cow that mooed softly while chewing some blades of grass pulled out of the uneven paving stones in the little courtyard.

With a quick movement, the little girl squeezed the cow's teats all the while rubbing with her other hand the udder filled with the good milk that squirted in a straight, linear stream toward the pail where the white liquid rose, frothy and fragrant.

Milk, real milk! Coralie had not seen it other than in cans, cartons or in a cup at breakfast. She marveled at this gift of nature, and while Madame Arsène collected enough milk to make her stock of dous lèt*, milk candy, for the week, Coralie always obtained a liter of the creamy, rich liquid she brought to Robert on her Sunday visit to Lise Alphonsin's home.*

The child liked her a lot, clapping his hands when seeing her approach with some inexpensive little toy, calling her Auntie Cora and hugging her nicely when she came and when she left, feeling surprised that his "Auntie" always held him a little too tightly against her chest.

Coralie had five calm years. Slowly, the hard way, she had learned to work, support herself financially, appreciate a simple, orderly life, and be content with the thousand little blessings that make up the joy of the humble. And she began to hope again.

At work, she had become a forewoman, then a supervisor, and found herself entrusted with more and more responsibilities by the boss who appreciated her efficiency, excellent manners, and the humane way she treated workers and personnel.

And it was then that bad luck, jealous of this overly tranquil, overly arduous, overly redeeming life, came knocking again at Coralie's door.

One day when she was trying with a worker to get the perforating machine working again, the motor started to race, the punch leapt into her right hand and began perforating it at an accelerated rhythm. In the time that it took to cut the current, Coralie, her hand chopped and loosing blood, had fainted from the pain.

Her wounds healed slowly, and the hand remained paralyzed. She had not lost any fingers and appeared normal, but her fingers stayed stiff and appeared fused together, unable to bend. This right hand, so indispensable in her work, was lost. Only the thumb was still mobile.

The boss kept her position for her for three months paying her all of her salary, but when it was established that poor Coralie would never recover the use of her right hand, she was nicely thanked with a compensation allowing her to hold out three more months. With what she had been able to save, she wanted to enter into a partnership with Madame Arsène, but since Coralie was no longer working, the shopkeeper, worried about her money, kept her at a distance.

The day came when Coralie was not able to pay for her little room. Without resources, she increased her expenses by resorting again to alcohol and tobacco, the only relief from the distress besetting her.

Ages ago, Marceau Santeuil, having assumed control of the Nivel Import Export Company, had become aware of the small irregularities that had allowed August Percier to give Coralie some help. He was immediately dismissed and, out of respect for his record of service, given an early retirement pension.

Coralie found herself approaching her fiftieth birthday without any resources because the subsidies that Lise Alphonsin had given her from time to time were slim and undependable. Besides, how could she ask anymore of a person who had assumed full support of her son Robert?

The evening of the day Madame Arsène evicted her from her lodgings, Coralie, with her pitiful bags, wandered around aimlessly and, at nightfall, she pushed open, almost automatically, the door of a cafe that she used to frequent at the time of her wild nights with Marcel Sibert.

The owner of the "Acapulco Bar" had not forgotten the beautiful, society woman who drank her liquor straight and danced until dawn. She explained her distress to him and asked him to rent her a room for one or two nights. The owner listened to her while shaking his head. Then, he offered her room and board, in exchange for ....

In exchange for ... One hour later, Coralie had her first "client."

FOURTEEN

And Coralie settled into this life of a prostitute. Wherever she went, she found herself bouzen kafe, a whore in a brothel. In spite of her effort to lead the life of an honest worker, she had eventually failed in her attempt to redeem herself in the eyes of the world and in her own eyes.

Now, she was totally exhausted. After her nights of paid love, she slept until noon, got up reluctantly, and, like an automate, ate the meal provided by the proprietor-pimp. She then went back to bed again lighting up cigarette after cigarette. In the twirls of smoke that rose to the ceiling, Coralie re-examined her past life. Her painful childhood, Aline's persecution, her ineffectual marriage eventually saved by Nivel's goodness, then life in France, the days at Deauville, the sojourns at Biarritz, the races at Auteuil, the first-class dinners with Klaus von Dieter at the Tour d'Argent and at Maxim's, the jewels, the dresses by Maggy Rouff, by Lanvin, the exquisite shoes from Bally or those signed André, the murmurs of admiration when, at the wheel of a Delahaye or a Panhard, she moved among the elegant women of her day in a white organdy dress and a flowery sun-hat.

Was it possibly she, the woman lying in the bed of this bare room in a brothel in Carrefour on this unpleasant, faded, heavy cotton bedspread with old prints on the walls and outdated calendars on which Marilyn Monroe stretched out to infinity her long, pin-up girl legs for soldiers' phantasms?

Was it possibly she who was going to get dressed toward six o'clock again this evening, and perched on a tall stool, at the bar, cigarette holder in her mouth, perfumed with "cheap" Madame Ganot, her leg sheathed in black, her skirt slit to reveal an inexpensive lace garter? Was it possibly she awaiting the "client" with whom she would go to ape the gestures and movements of love for a ten or twenty dollar bill that she would pop into her bra or into her shoe?

Was it possibly she, this prostitute who bragged about making more "passes" than the other boarders in the brothel because, although a lot older than her rivals, she had an air of distinction, an aristocratic bearing that attracted common customers only too happy to sleep with the society woman turned lady of the night?

Was it possibly she, Coralie Nivel, who found herself all day long exposed to the jealousy of the women from the Dominican Republic who called her, by alluding to her stiffened hand, Cora la Manca, the half-handed Cora which was somehow much nicer than the nicknames that the Haitian prostitutes or servants attributed to her.

Because of her pale eyes, the latter had nicknamed her Chwal Je Dajan, Horse with Silver Eyes while her irritated rivals, for the disdainful air that she sported well in spite of herself, alas, flung at her as she passed by compliments like Coralie Men Pòk, Coralie Crippled Hand. Then her still reddish blond hair merited the nicknames Allumette Bengale, Sparkler, Foumi Kako, the Rebel Ant, Gengenbrette Lakòl, Sticky Ginger.

But at this point, Cora was well beyond distress, beyond destiny. Everything glided over her; she gave in to her fate without any sort of struggle other than that of the most rudimentary survival. So when last week, a vendor had treated her like a bouzen pyès, a cheap prostitute, because she hesitated to pay the high price for a pair of dark glasses intended to hide the black eye given her by an overly drunk customer, she had smiled sadly at the salesman without answering him back and returned to the brothel to care for her swollen eye with herbal hot packs.

And mechanically, like drinking or walking, Coralie continued this life of a derelict, a societal reject, an outcast. Sleep, rising, meals, cigarettes, washing, dressing, customers until exhausted, her head empty and buzzing, her legs shaking, she eventually fell fully dressed onto the bed with its questionable odors for a deep, dreamless sleep.

And the cycle resumed, infernal, without exit, a tunnel where life, in spite of herself, had caught her.

And the days passed in this way for Cora, the prostitute. She only went to see Robert very infrequently at Lise Alphonsin's house. The doctor had stuck to her word, and the adolescent now knew who his real mother was. Life had frustrated Coralie, and it was she who now felt unworthy of the name of mother, and she was upset with herself for having to face the innocent look of the child she had cherished so much and for desecrating this smooth forehead with a kiss tainted with too many impure caresses.

Coralie was fifty-six years old when the 1957 events broke out. At the slightest provocation, the people of Port-au-Prince, beautiful neighborhoods and sordid outlying sections combined, threw themselves into the streets to take part in the general upheaval. Insecurity at night cut down the number of clients at the brothel, and the girls, less busy, woke up earlier and had freer days, and sometimes in search of diversion, joined the excited observers.

So it was that on May 25, 1957, the confrontation at the Dessalines Barracks found poor Coralie in a group of sight-seers who had come to the Champ de Mars to witness the battle.

A stray shell flattened a row of spectators, among them Coralie whose face was wounded by the shrapnel, while a second piece, lodged between her two vertebra, damaging her spinal chord.

Coralie, her jaw shattered, spent six months in General Hospital. At first, they thought she would never be able to walk again. And it was a miracle when she could take several steps on the arms of her sister-companions who served, one after the other, as her nurses. Curiously enough, these flowers from the brothel felt that when she was out of the hospital, Coralie would never again be a serious rival to them in their nightly business. So they cared for her devotedly. There was always one of them there at Coralie's side to help her in the communal dining room. They brought her food every day, washed and dressed her, combed her long hair which had become gray, cut her nails, powdered her, perfumed her, and told her all of the good stories that made the rounds in the main room and bedrooms at the house of ill-repute.

Cora couldn't help laughing at these women's liveliness and was touched by their kindness to her. She had seen little of Lise who said that she didn't want to expose Robert to the shock of seeing his mother in such bad shape. So she stopped by two or three times solely to provide medications needed for her old friend's treatment.

At the end of six months, when Coralie was finally able to leave the hospital, held up by two affectionate prostitutes, she tried out for the first time that strange, jerky walk that from then on was to be hers and which was going to earn her the nickname Janm Debwa, Wooden Legs, matching that of Djòl Kase, Broken Jaw, a clever allusion to her lopsided jaw.

The arrival at the "Acapulco" was a triumph. They installed Cora in a rocking chair as she got out of the taxi, and she was carried as if she were on a palanquin by the boarders and the servants as far as a tiny, little room on the courtyard reserved for her; here for several days, she was cared for and pampered much better than at the hospital. The proprietor was kind-hearted and was not going to throw a poor creature into the street who had had her hours of ephemeral glory in his establishment. Men tou sa pa sa, but after all, Coralie was costing him a lot to feed, and he had to find her a job so that she stopped being a burden to his business. The boarders held council and decided that, instead of personnally taking care of their intimate apparel demanding thorough and frequent washing, they would entrust the care of their undergarments, lingerie, and dressing gowns to Cora. It is in this way that Coralie went from the status of an active member of the brothel's chattels to that of private laundress for the women. Coralie learned to wash in spite of her main pòk, her crippled hand and to iron by holding the iron in her left hand. She learned to like this modest work but every now and then she still had to resume her former job when a client, who was almost completely broke, asked the proprietor for an available, inexpensive prostitute.

Coralie no longer felt the humiliation of her condition. Like dlo mennen, van pouse, water pushed by the wind, she lived her unfortunate life indifferent to the gibes and jeers which broke out in her path. Djòl Kase, Chwal Je Dajan, Janm Debwa, Coralie la Manca, Po Lanvè, Blemished Skin, Bale Joudlan, New Year's Broom. Now nothing touched her.

With a trace of modesty, in order to avoid the passes of penniless chauffeurs or poverty stricken vendors, she asked to live alone. The proprietor found her a little clay room in Waney, a shanty town, a lakou, a courtyard, owned by Mr. Elifaite Tibidon and his son, Cétoute. The owners were tough but honest, and as long as renters paid regularly, they left them completely alone and did not pry into their private lives.

Every week, Coralie went down in a taxi to pick up the laundry of the women at the Acapulco Bar and went back up the same way. Then, still by taxi, she went as far as Rivière Froide to wash the dance-hall women's laundry in the beautiful, clear water. In her neighborhood at Waney, she also found some customers who entrusted their sheets and pillowcases to her because she had a good reputation for laundering fine and delicate garments.

With this schedule, she maintained her physical life devoid of all joy, all hope. Coralie Santeuil was truly dead. All that remained was "Cora Laundry" as the customers called her.

And did it not just so happen that even that was going to fail her. Where and how did she catch that cursed fungus that devoured her fingernails and penetrated her flesh?

Her fingertips became stumps tinged with blood which, when she tried to rub the laundry more, should she catch them on a button or the hook of a bra, became open sores shedding ugly, puss-filled drops. She tried rightly to hire a helper to wash for her while she continued to do the ironing. But in order to iron, she had to press down very hard on the iron, and the painful fingertips of her diseased hands did not enable her to continue.

So when at the Hôpital Adventiste at 63 Diquini Street, she was told that she must never again touch either detergent or laundry soap and that she must totally stop using them or risk amputation, she understood that life was over for her, and that all she had left to do was lie down and die.

Fortunately, her rent at Waney was paid for six months until December 31 thanks to the last gift from Lise who still supported her although somewhat irregularly. Perhaps if she had had the means to transport herself downtown more easily, she would have been able to go to Lise's clinic on the Chemin des Dalles to be more regularly treated, but she could not tolerate any more hassle or fatigue. Hardships had made her thinner, paler. Her hair, roughly cut with a dull knife, hung irregularly around her scarred face. A strange, quiet smile deformed the bottom of her face in a permanent sneer making people afraid. Her pèpè *clothes, some used clothing from Mrs. Dieufils, were wretched and became veritable rags due to the overly frequent washing done unwillingly for her by Céphise, the good woman's goddaughter, an unpleasant girl who always grumbled upon seeing Coralie.*

"Han, men ravèt blanch la ap vini ak de ran dan l pou l manje manje nennenn mwen. Wi m rayi madam pye sech sa a. *Hey, here is that white cockroach coming with nothing but teeth to eat my god-mother's food. Oh yes, I sure hate that stick-legged woman.*"

Coralie had only one less shabby, more decent dress to put on, and that is the one she would wear the next day to go to ask for rent money for the next six months that she must pay without fail on January 1 to Cétoute Tibidon who held his father's purse strings and who pa pran priyè, *was not moved by pity.*

Cora looked with a vacant stare at the woven plastic shoes given to her by Magritte, that former friend from the brothel who no longer wanted to see her since she had become a madan marye, *a married woman. They were a little tight for her, but they would hold up. Tomorrow, December 31, she would have a lot of walking to do.*

Tomorrow ….

Saint Sylvester, pray for Coralie the crippled woman whose life slips away like a handful of water ….

THE THIRTEENTH STATION

JANUARY 1: DELMAS

2:00 A.M.

The New Year's Eve party at the Nivels is in full swing. At the sound of midnight, they heard the traditional cannon shot, and they competed with one another to embrace, some lips lingering longer than acceptable on consenting cheeks.

Colonel Darcourt took advantage of the moment to press Solanges Nivel against himself while murmuring to her:

"I love you. I love you, Sol ..., my sun ...."

Solanges returned the brief embrace without a word, but in such an already unconstrained way that her ploy did not escape her two friends. Madame Rosenblum, a beautiful, part-Jewish woman with a ferocious humor, leaned toward the ear of Angèle Pitou, a chubby little woman who laughs constantly:

"I say, Angèle, it looks as if everything is going along just fine between Darcourt and Solanges. We could very well say ...."

"Look at Nivel's long face. If looks could kill, Darcourt would be dead."

"Are you surprised? Darcourt looks like a man who is going to "niveler," "level" the woman rather soon."

At the word "niveler," which she finds extremely amusing, Angèle Pitou breaks into a shrill laugh that makes everybody turn their heads.

Embarrassed, she puts her hand over her mouth and stops dead. But no matter what, the pun is good, and she spreads it around. A week later, all of Port-au-Prince will know that Madame Nivel got herself "nivelée," "leveled" by the handsome officer, even if nothing had happened yet.

At the present time, they are dancing beneath subdued lights. Lovingly clasped in one another's arms in the midst of other couples, Solanges and Pierre Darcourt form but a single body. Uneasy, the woman steps aside:

"Pierre, be careful. My husband is watching us."

"Sol, tell me, tell me quickly, my darling. I'm madly in love with you. When? When?"

In a breath, Solanges murmurs:

"Tomorrow at five o'clock, at your place."

Pierre Darcourt is ecstatic. He finally has a rendezvous with Solanges, a rendezvous during which he is going to possess this enticing dark beauty whom he has desired for months.

This evening, she is irresistible in a white dress covered with silver spangles which hugs her sculptural body without hiding any of her charms. He is thinking when the dance finishes:

"Ala yon bèl nègès! What a beautiful woman! What a gorgeous Black beauty!"

The dancer steps back from his partner, openly kisses her hand, and takes his leave. It is two o'clock in the morning. He has nothing else to do at the Nivels. He has obtained this promise, this certitude that he had come looking for, determined as he was to extract consent from the woman he desired so much.

Tomorrow morning, he has several duties. He will have to get up very early for the Te Deum at which he must, in spite of everything, appear. On January first, Independence Day, all the government officials, the president in the lead, will have caroused all night long and, bundled up in their winter attire, white shirts and dark suits, their heads will nod ever so nicely. But it is the custom. They will all be there. After that, they will go to sleep for a good, long time. Darcourt, in his handsome dress uniform with epaulettes and shoulder-braid will have been noticed by more than one woman in attendance, but he will be thinking only about Solanges, about the heavenly promise:

"Tomorrow at five o'clock, at your place."

And he takes off into the night at the wheel of his Mercedes Benz 330SL. He loves this car whose power merges with the energy he feels surging in himself. His jaw clenched, Darcourt speeds into the night on Delmas 60. He is going to take the highway because he lives in La Plaine.

Like a jaguar, the vehicle leaps into the chilly, tropical winter night.

On the return road, Coralie Santeuil strolls slowly along Delmas Avenue in the pale January night. She no longer feels her fatigue and her infirmity. After having created her to be "the perfect image" of misfortune, destiny offers her a belated compensation to be sure, but also an exemplary one. She piled up mistakes on top of errors, she ruined her life by being ill prepared, frivolous, flighty, and improvident. But now on the horizon of her lonely, penniless old age, the dawn of a new life appears. A life redeemed by the rediscovered love of her son Robert and the portended tenderness of the sweet Magali. Robert will have to get married some day; he will have children, and other joyful mouths will call her "grandmother." How she will spoil them, how she will love them! And then, who knows, Magali, so gracious and good, will perhaps marry soon enough so that she, Coralie, the outcast, the reviled one, may have the joy of knowing her great-grandchildren.

Frightfully old, disfigured, Coralie tells herself that it is not too late. She no longer fears this "too late" which resonated like a death knoll throughout her tumultuous life. She has paid for the right to catch a glimpse of a dignified, decent life filled with the calm blessing granted one's later days with her beauty, her best years, her suffering.

A strange peace floods the poor woman's heart. A blissful euphoria washes completely over her. Never in her miserable existence has she felt such peace and hope for happiness within herself.

Once at Delmas 60, Coralie decides to change paths. The road is deserted, cars very rare. The revelers are not yet ready to go home. Only several isolated gun shots puncture the clear night. It is New Year's Day. A new year, a new life are beginning for Coralie, the redeemed one, who carries within her today the gentle burden of human love she has finally encountered.

Coralie moves forward to cross the deserted artery ...

■ ■ ■ ■ ■

Absorbed in the ecstasy of thinking about Solanges' disconcerting body, Colonel Darcourt has, for a infinitesimal fraction of a second, let his mind wander to the passionately desired meeting with this woman who drives his senses crazy. Tomorrow, rather today, later on, shortly. He does not realize that he is accelerating instead of slowing down, and he misses the descending curve, hits the right shoulder, swerves, straightens out the protesting car too abruptly ....

And there is a sudden impact. Inevitable.

Like a disjointed puppet, a human body literally flies into the air projected by the force of the racing car. Yet he had applied the breaks, applied them as hard as he could, almost losing control of the car in a rollover.

He succeeds in stopping sixty feet down the road. He gets out of the car. What a blow! He will have to pick up this body, take it to the hospital, alert the insurance company, perhaps assume the care needed for his victim over whom he now leans anxiously ….

During his military career, Darcourt has seen too many cadavers to be wrong. The woman who lies there, her skull lying against the dip in the road, is dead, truly dead. There is nothing more to be done for Coralie.

What good will it do to attend to her, since it is obvious that there is nothing more to do. Darcourt hesitates a moment which seemed like an hour, yet as a matter of fact, he makes up his mind in few seconds. Why burden himself with complications because of a poor, old woman struck by accident on a deserted road? Somebody will surely discover the cadaver at dawn and will alert the hospital which will send an ambulance. What does one more dead woman and one less poor person matter to the Republic?

Darcourt gets back behind the steering wheel of the Mercedes. He has not gone a hundred meters before he is already pushing down on the accelerator and the powerful car springs again into the night. He has already forgotten the passerby. He is thinking only about Solanges and about her promise.

Oh you who pardoned Mary Magdalene, take pity on Coralie, the sinner who died this morning, her heart filled with an immense love.

▪ ▪ ▪ ▪ ▪

At the service station at the lower end of the Delmas road, a black Mercedes enters like a whirlwind making its tires squeal. Nervous, irritable, the driver gets out and slams the car door with an angry gesture. He walks around his vehicle, looks at the front bumper, the right fender, and, furious, exclaims:

"Hell! Gade jan fanm nan kolboso machin nèf mwen an. Look what this woman did to my brand new car."

Furious both with himself and with his victim, he beats on the cabin door of the night attendant who wakes up haggard from his sleep and staggers out:

"Banm ven dola gaz epi suye maching nan ban mwen. Give me twenty dollars worth of gas and wipe off my car."

The man wakes up under the domineering voice which he senses is in the habit of giving orders. The client is wearing civilian clothes, but everything about his gestures reveals the military: his appearance, his voice, his abrupt gestures.

The tank filled, the man takes a rag and begins the task of wiping off the car.

"Fè vit. M prese, souke kò w. Do it quickly. I'm in a hurry. Get moving."

The man rushes.

"Suye defans devan an. Wipe off the front bumper."

The guy bends over and wipes, and it is then that he sees, his eyes wide with terror, a lock of gray hair caked on by something that looks like yellowish butter.

"Letènel, li fèk tiye yon moun ... Good God, he has just killed someone ...."

The attendant's frightened look has met the colonel's dry, cold eyes.

And the man lowers his head and suddenly gets busy and rubs ... and rubs.

The colonel gives him a large bill. It is thirty dollars more than needed for the sale of the gasoline. Perhaps so that the attendant will remain silent, if by chance, someday, they were to question him.

But who will ever dare to question him?

And the Mercedes takes off again toward La Plaine. The opaque night swallows up the black arrow that shoots off under the motor's full power.

Far away on the road, up there, like a tall disjointed marionette, Coralie Santeuil sleeps. At last.

Her passage on this earth is over.

THE FOURTEENTH STATION

JANUARY FIRST, RUE MONSEIGNEUR GUILLOUX

6:00 A.M.

Origène Petigène, stretcher-bearer by profession at the General Hospital, is finishing his night duty. The routine for January first. Some revelers will never celebrate anything anymore because, in the euphoria which welcomes a new year, there are always nuts who kill each other with stray bullets or knives. Origène is nonchalant. He has taken on this duty for ten years, and on this night alone, he has already received two or three cadavers killed with bullets and one stabbed with an ice pick.

"Yo pap goute sèl ankò. Zafè yo. They won't be tasting salt anymore. That's their business. As for me, the head of the family, how could I even think about *pren yon ti gwòg, fè yon ti fèt,* about having a drink or having a party since things are going so badly for me," thinks Origène.

A wife, two children in school, a salary of two hundred gourdes. Two hundred gourdes cut each month by Solidarité, ONA, CLE, Péligre and other nameless indirect taxes. What is left for him to nourish, dress, and shelter his family? It is true that his wife, Adélia, is plucky and hard working. She crosses the city with fabric remnants on her head and on her arms, holding a shortened yard stick under her left armpit. But so many women have this same business that they must sometimes sell on credit, and one fine day, they notice that the *pratique,* the regular customer has taken off without paying, and that it is a total loss eating up the slim profits.

How is he going to tackle the month of January beginning today? Like all state employees, he received his meager salary on December seventeenth or eighteenth for the feast of Christmas. What feast? He could not even buy a little plastic toy for Junior, his ten year old son; not even *yon ti pope fil pou Mariana,* a little rag doll for Mariana, his ever so charming little girl who will soon be seven. He had to think about serious things, big responsibilities, absolutely necessary shoes for school, paying the grocer who always grants credit, but who does not hesitate to "demean" the defaulting customer. Once that is taken care of and the rent paid, Origène cannot buy himself *menm yon kòd tabak,* a little bit of tobacco.

Yes, January … Everybody knows that January se *demwa ki kontre,* is like two months in one. How to continue this difficult month among others? How to begin this new year without resources? *Adélia pral babye nan tèt li jouk mwa a bout.* Adélia is going to complain until the month is over. Origène sighs. He is certainly going to have to approach his wife this morning. He is not going to be able to bring back *cinq centimes kwiv,* one red cent. *Kote li ta pran?* Where will he find it …?

An ambulance, its siren howling, enters the hospital's courtyard. It unloads its quota of dead bodies. Among them there is a little girl stuck by a stray bullet. They noted in time she is not completely dead.

There is a small, well-dressed young man who received a long knife wound in his stomach and who is obviously deader than a door-nail ….

There is a third cadaver that looks like a beggar and Origène wonders:

"O yon fanm blanch. Kòman li fè vin nan eta sa a? Oh, a white woman. How did she end up in this condition?"

In the young man's pocket, they found an identification card, and the employee is busy arduously copying the name on the tag to be attached to the corpse.

Then, he examines the other one, the old woman with the shattered skull. Nothing. Not a single paper, no identification, no pockets, no handbag.

He will affix the tag routinely used at l'Hopital Général for a female who cannot speak: (F.S.P.) Femme Sans Parole. With his clumsy hand, he does his utmost to mark on a label, putting out his tongue:

"January I, 19 ..., 6:00 A.M., *inconi ajeu 70 ans apeprè,* unidentified old woman, about 70 years of age."

That is how he has been taught to do it. The two dead people are quickly undressed and their descriptive labels attached to their right big toe with a tightly knotted string. And Origène, who is strong, loads the cadavers on a wheeled stretcher, the woman underneath, the man on top.

And on to the morgue. After that, his duty finished, he will go home to la Rue Muller, the first avenue in Bolosse, and all day long he will not even be able to rest as Adélia is going to talk so much, a lot, always complaining about money. Yes, *li toujou ap baye pou zafè lajan,* she always complains about money.

Origène finds a place for the young man who has a surprised look on his face as if he had been amazed to recognize the one who struck him. Perhaps a scuffle over some whore. There he is, well behaved forever in the future.

Then it is the turn of the poor white-looking woman who appears to smile on one side of her face. Origène is putting her away as best he can in a drawer already occupied by a little, old man when he notices that the dead woman has her left fist closed on something reddish which may well be a five gourde bill, a dollar bill. At least, with that, Origène will be able to pay for some biscuits and a good cup of coffee before going back home.

And he begins the task of opening the fingers contracted from rigor mortis.

He has to break them. The forced finger joints make a crackling sound as they are broken, and it is a five hundred gourde bill, a hundred U.S. dollar bill, folded into quarters that appears. Origène cannot believe his eyes.

"Jesus, Mary, and Joseph, *gade yon zetrenn! Mesye* ... what a New Year's gift! Man ...."

And he makes the sign of the cross two times, three times in a row, beats his breast, and looks at the dead woman who seems to smile at him.

"*Mèsi, mèsi anpil, vye namnam,* Thanks, thanks a lot, dear old mother."

Now he is in a hurry to get home. Before arriving at his house, he is going to go to the little market at the lower end of First Avenue to get a good supply of food. He is going to buy dried herring, two trays of biscuits, avocados, oil, eggs. What a tasty meal Adélia is going to prepare for them this New Year's Day morning! And how happy she will be when he gives her a dress and a scarf plus a bottle of *santibon,* a bottle of perfume on top of everything else! And he will still have enough to pay for the children's schooling for the coming months of January and February.

His heart bursting with gratitude, he heaves a sigh of relief and say again in petto:

"*Mèsi, mèsi anpil vye manman, map lapriyè pou ou, pou Bondye pran ou nan paradi.* Thanks, thanks, dear mama. I'll pray for you so God will take you into paradise."

Origène Petigène changed his spotted smock for his old coat hanging on a hook close to the entrance door. He waves to the other employees who are still drowsy.

"*Mesye, m ale wi. A demen. Epi Bòn Ane* .... *Bon Ane tout moun.* Guys, I'm leaving. See you tomorrow. Happy New Year ... Happy New Year to everyone."

"*Bòn Ane, Kamarad.* Happy New Year, my friends."

Raising the collar of his shabby coat because of the cool air, he pushes the gate open. In the bottom of his pocket, the man fingers the blessed bill and feels its still new texture as he thinks about his family's good fortune.

And whistling happily, Origène Petigène plunges into the dawning day.

ACKNOWLEDGMENTS

I wish to express my deep appreciation to all those who have contributed in one way or another to the present publication, a translation of my novel—*Le Passage*—which will now be available to an English speaking audience under the title, *Vale of Tears*.

My heartfelt thanks go first to my translator and friend, Dr. Dolores A. Schaefer of St. Paul, Minnesota, who has devoted years to translate the book from an albeit difficult French—and from many passages written in Haitian Creole—to perfect English; her dedication to my work was an endeavor of great love for Haitian literature. Professor Joelle Vitiello of Macalaster College in Minnesota assisted Dr. Schaefer with the translation of sections written in Haitian Creole. I am very appreciative to her for doing so and also for going over the entire manuscript.

My deep gratitude goes to my dear friend and colleague, Dr. Carrol Coates of Binghamton University, a long-time promoter of Haitian literature in the United States and a strong supporter of my own work. He was the first to translate a section of my novel—*Le Creuset*—for a special issue of *Callaloo*. Dr. Coates read over this translation and his impeccable knowledge of the three languages was for us a great asset. As we were all grappling with how to translate *Le Passage* into English, my daughter noticed in one of Carrol's email, the expression "vale of tears" which he used to stress that the title needed to emphasize the many tribulations and sufferings throughout Coralie Santueil's life of misery. We finally felt that we had found the right title for the English version of the book—*Vale of Tears*. This is just one of Carrol's many contributions to this work.

I am very fortunate for the help received from Professors Helen Pyne-Timothy and Douglas Henry Daniels from the Department of Black Studies at the University of California, Santa Barbara. They both made very useful suggestions as the work was undergoing final revision. I am grateful to my grand-daughter, Kyrah Daniels, who provided great assistance during the last stage of the project.

I am indebted to Bill Murray who, upon reading it, liked the book immediately and worked so diligently to find an editor interested in publishing in English a story so typically Haitian; and to my current publisher, Farhad Shirzad of *Ibex Publishers*, who so gallantly took the cultural risk of launching *Vale of Tears* for an American audience. Taraneh Taghizadeh, Farzin Yazdanfar and Susanne Knopp must be acknowledged and thanked for their careful reading and comments. I also thank Hërsza Barjon for the use of her beautiful artwork on the cover.

Warm thanks also to my editors in Haiti, *Les Editions Le Natal* and to Robert Malval and his staff who did such a good job with the publication of the French version of the book in spite of the many difficulties that editing and printing entail in Haiti.

I also wish to express my appreciation to other colleagues also working to promote Haiti and Haitian literature in the United States. Among them are Dr. Patrick Bellegarde-Smith of the University of Wisconsin-Milwaukee who, in the tradition of my dear friend, his grand-father, the late Dantès Bellegarde, continues to do such important work for Haiti and Dr. Anne Paulette Smith of Tufts University to whom I am infinitely grateful for the article she wrote on my work for *AFRICANA, The Encyclopedia of the African American Experience*. Also to the women of the *Multicultural Women's Press* in Florida—Drs. Marlène Racine-Toussaint, Florence Bellande-Robertson and Régine Latortue—for their wonderful initiative and their determination to promote *les lettres haitiennes* in the United States.

This acknowledgment would not be complete without my thanking my young colleague and friend, the brilliant novelist, Edwidge Danticat, Haiti's most prestigious literary ambassador in the international community for writing a foreword to this book. I must also acknowledge the Center for Black Studies at the University of California, Santa Barbara for promoting work on Haiti and for publishing the *Journal of Haitian Studies*. My appreciation goes likewise to the *Haitian Studies Association*.

Last but not least, my heartfelt thanks and full gratitude to my beloved daughter, Dr. Claudine Michel, a professor in the Department of Black Studies at the University of California, Santa Barbara, whose devotion to my work and filial perseverance has rendered possible this long delayed publication.

To all of them, I reiterate my deepest gratitude.

Paulette Poujol-Oriol
Port-au-Prince, Haiti
January 7, 2002

AFTERWORD

PAULETTE POUJOL ORIOL … IN PERSON!

Over eleven years ago, I picked up a copy of Paulette Poujol Oriol's first novel, *Le Creuset*, from a Haitian book importer and read it with fascination. Although my scanty knowledge of Kreyòl was insufficient to fully appreciate the exchange of insults between two antagonistic mothers, Mansia and Dégrâce, the French text was enough to send me looking for Haitian students and friends to help me understand the dialogue, including Dégrâce's scathing comment that little Roro's father was a Panyòl (Dominican) who had disappeared. Watching the older generation pulling each other's hair and wrestling, the boys soon forget their own disagreement. The fight ends with the stout Mansia lifting Dégrâce up and hurling her to the ground, only to rush to the aid of her suffering neighbor a moment later. Paulette's story was gripping and funny in spite of details in the dialogue that were opaque for a non-Haitian reader.

Some time later (1993), Paulette came to visit, speaking first to students and colleagues at Binghamton University before I drove her to Boston for an appearance in the special series of talks focused on Haitian women writers at the Cambridge Public Library. I was amazed to discover that Haitian students here already knew about Paulette because had heard the rebroadcasts (in the New York City area) of her former radio comedy series originally broadcast in Port-au-Prince with the collaboration of Paulette, her daughter, Claudine Michel, and writer Mona Guérin. In Cambridge, Paulette was greeted with an enthusiastic reception both by new readers and former students who had not seen her for years.

Readers who are not widely familiar with Haitian literature should know there is a history of diverse writing by Haitian women, from the novels of the early 1930s by Cléanthe Desgraves (Mme. Virgile Valcin), *Cruelle destinée* and *La blanche négresse*, and Annie Desroy (Mme. Étienne Bourand), *Le joug*, to the younger generations now publishing, including Edwidge Danticat, who has made a name for herself writing in English. Like their male counterparts, few Haitian women have enjoyed the benefits offered by major publishers, in particular, more extensive publicity and distribution. The majority of Haitian women writing in French, have been constrained to see their own work through printing and limited distribution, a mark of the minimal and precarious existence of the book industry in Haiti. Lack of systematic publicity and serious criticism means many worthwhile works of fiction remain virtually unknown, awaiting discovery by inquiring connoisseurs.

Paulette Poujol Oriol's *Le Creuset* received one of the few literary distinctions offered in Haiti, the Prix Deschamps for 1980, which brought publication by the Deschamps publishing firm. The major Paris newspaper, *Le Monde*, recognized the story "*La Fleur rouge*" (later published in a volume of stories by the same title) as the best francophone short story in the 1988 competition. English-speaking readers have had only a minimal possibility of getting acquainted with Paulette's exceptional story-telling talent (in the spring 1992 issue of *Callaloo*, I published an excerpt from Le creuset).

The publication of *Vale of Tears (Le passage)* in an excellent English translation by Dolores A. Schaefer is the occasion for anglophone readers to become acquainted with a novel that is likely to elicit tears and anger. I leave it to future critics to interpret the implicitly religious framework Paulette has given the story of Coralie Santeuil's path from bourgeois comfort to absolute misery by segmenting her narrative into fourteen alternating chapters and "Stations" (of the Cross ...!), alternative leaps from present to past and back. Leaving aside also the question of an eventual evaluation of Paulette Poujol Oriol's standing among Haitian fiction writers, I want to suggest that she is a *konpozè* in the traditional sense of a mesmerizing story-teller/poet who draws her readers/listeners into living the fictional experience through her command of drama and language. In her brief "Introductory Remarks," Paulette notes that *Vale of Tears* is the result of having accepted the challenge of telling a story different from that of *Le creuset*, where the little fighter of the opening gradually, and improbably, makes his way out of the slums of Tètbèf to become a well-known doctor and founder of a children's hospital. The Coralie of *Vale of Tears* comes of a bourgeois family and, in her naiveté, she falls victim to the machinations of her stepmother. She is unable to reverse her downward course from the moment she finds herself dispossessed by the stepmother to her final days as an out-of-work prostitute and bag lady.

Let readers be outraged and, at the same time, appreciative of the powerful story-telling talent of Paulette Poujol Oriol.

— Carrol F. Coates
Binghamton, 10 June 2002

Made in the USA
Middletown, DE
11 April 2018